BLOOD
& BRUTE
& GINGER ROOT

MELISSA WRIGHT

BLOOD
& BRUTE
& GINGER
ROOT

PROLOGUE

Miles woke in a cold sweat, the feel of icy fingers crawling over his bare flesh. He stared at the ceiling of his bedroom while he worked to steady his breathing. It had not been the first time he'd startled awake, sensations clawing through the haze of his memory and into his waking world. But those dreams had been of fire and screaming, of his brothers lost to the flame. This was something else entirely.

He ran a hand over his chest, the strangest sensation still lingering there. He thought he caught the scent of cinnamon and something earthy in his bedroom, but he could not focus on what in the dim light of dawn. All he could do was think of her, the dark eyes and windblown hair of stranger, ethereal and—impossibly—all too real. She had whispered something in the darkness, words that Miles could not understand, then her palm had opened and a dozen rose petals had spilled free.

His phone chimed, and Miles took one final, shaky breath before pushing the tangled sheets free of his legs to sit off the edge of the bed. He picked up the phone to find a message from Tommy, a warning about a coming storm. "We've escalated to weather reports now?" Miles muttered, dropping the device back onto the empty nightstand on his way the shower. He turned on the faucet full blast, steam coating the glass surround as he stared in the mirror at a face that had suffered too little sleep. Tommy had been pestering him ever since the building collapse, urging Miles to see someone, to talk about the dreams. But Miles hadn't. He'd been convinced he could work through it, that they would eventually become less severe.

It had been three years. Last night was the first that had not ended in flames. A car drove by outside, too fast, its radio blaring over the sound of the shower, Santana crooning about a black magic woman, begging her not to turn her back on him. Miles shook his head, turning from the mirror to peel his boxers off, but something slipped beneath his foot on the tile floor. He plucked it from the floor, then lifted it gingerly to examine. Steam swelled through the room, along with his disbelief.

Pinched between his fingers, a single, bright red rose petal waited. The same as was in the dream. Miles could only stare, and that petal—ominous as it was—seemed to stare right back at him.

1

———

Diana Coulton had withered under the censorious gaze of her cat for the last time. She was swearing off tequila, and that was that.

Diana, not the cat. The cat had given up drinking ages ago.

Prue looked up from her condemnation, tail swishing, as Diana's sister trudged in through the back of the shop.

"Are you cooking up something for this hangover?" Belle's mascara was smudged, her dark hair askew. She rubbed a palm over her face. "My head is pounding."

Diana laughed and then winced at her own throbbing skull. "It's nearly done."

Belle climbed onto a stool, laying head and torso onto the herb-scattered worktable with a groan. Diana resisted the urge to ask her what she'd put into their margaritas. The way she felt, she wasn't sure she ever wanted to know.

Besides, she'd had an ill feeling since she'd rolled out of bed and refused to go back to the subject they'd gotten into before they'd gone to sleep. "Have you seen Bernie?"

Belle lifted her head, two sage leaves and a bit of mint pressed into her cheek. The neck of her shirt was stretched, falling nearly off her shoulder, and Diana frowned. She was pretty sure it had been neatly folded in her own dresser the night before. Belle yawned. "That girl will be asleep all day. I heard her shuffling around at about three."

Diana handed her sister a warm mug, and Belle took it, managing a wan smile and a "cheers" as she clinked the rim to Diana's own. They tossed the concoction back quickly, not bothering to hide their matching grimaces, and Diana started the kettle for the morning tea. No matter that it was nearly one in the afternoon.

She wished she'd gotten a letter from their mother. She wished she could remember her hazy dream. She wished, not for the first time, she'd not let her sisters talk her into margaritas when there was work to be done.

Belle sighed, her fingers playing over the rim of her mug. "Better already. You, older sister, are a talent." She stood to stretch, raising her arms overhead so that her stolen shirt exposed a pair of unreasonably long thighs.

"There are boiled eggs in the icebox and fruit on the counter. Make sure you eat something before you go," Diana said.

Belle gave her side-eye, which she considered a more mature variation of her childhood go-to: the eye roll.

"I do not sound like somebody's mother," Diana said at the silent mocking. "If I had, I would have said, 'Arabelle Celeste Coulton, put on some pants this very instant or the devil take your magic!'"

Belle snorted. "Too real, Di. Too real."

"And if you happen to see Bernadette, remind her I need that list today. We have an order going out in the morning, and I can't keep holding off while she rummages around for her notes." Diana flicked a wayward rose petal—bright red and silky soft—off her shoulder, wondering where she'd picked it up.

Belle danced barefoot to the counter, standing on tiptoe as she lifted the lid of a glass apothecary jar and took out a licorice stick. She jerked a bite from the end before using it to point at the wall calendar. "What's with the heart?"

A strange chill ran over Diana's arms, and she turned, finding her pencil-only planner marked with giant red loops. "Is that permanent marker?"

Belle moved closer behind her. "Yep. Must be younger sister. Would've used lipstick if it were me."

"Why would Bernie mark the shop calendar? She has her own."

Diana could feel Belle shrug, but she couldn't seem to take her eyes from the blood-red heart. Its mark was in two days. At the full moon.

"I gotta tell ya," Belle said, tapping Diana's shoulder with her floppy licorice, "there's no way to know what's in that girl's head."

Diana nodded, turning in time to see Belle take another bite. She resisted the urge to remind her to chew with her mouth closed.

Belle smirked, nearly taunting her into it. "Such an easy target," she said. She leaned forward, smacking a licorice-scented kiss on her sister's cheek. "See you tomorrow, doll. Don't forget I'm taking Tuesday off."

"And why was that, again?" Diana said to her back.

All she heard was Belle's impish laugh.

Diana turned to the counter, gathering up the paperwork she'd left out the day before. Belle had traipsed into the workshop with a pitcher of margaritas before Diana had gotten the accounting finished, and between her and Bernie, they'd convinced her to take a Sister Saturday because they "hadn't had one in months." Diana had not been so sure, but as often happened under their influence, she'd agreed. Against her better judgment. And now she was working on a Sunday, when the Saturday Sisters were nowhere to be found.

The three had taken over the empty shop two years before, with big dreams and more than a few foolish assumptions. Diana had immediately volunteered to do the accounting and orders, and her sisters had agreed she should. They all knew Diana was the responsible one. It hadn't taken long to assign most of the important tasks as such, and in short order, she was running the business end of things on her own. While Diana loved the shop with all her heart, it rarely left her time for anything else. *Anything like men*, she started to think, but cut the errant thought off before it returned to the previous night's conversation. She refused to dwell on Bernie's idea that a "hot hunk of man" would somehow make Diana's life more complete.

She filed away the monthly reports, making notes about where they needed to focus the following quarter. They were making it, but Diana preferred to have a little more cushion in their accounts, just in case business were to slow. The herbs and supplies did well no matter the season, but books were more hit and miss. She would have loved to invest in more titles, but that required cash she wasn't ready to spend. So for now, Bad Medicine Books & Herbs held mostly older editions and special-order books and was heavy on the herbs portion of their namesake.

The "Bad" portion had been Bernie's idea. To share the

space with some part of them, even if it was only each of their initials: Bernadette, Arabelle, and Diana. Diana had painstakingly painted it onto the storefront banner in block print as Belle held the ladder and Bernie cheered them on. Her youngest sister was enthusiastic in many things and had a knack for growing. Bernie would spend hours upon hours in the work shed behind their family home, where she lived alone now that their parents were gone—absent in everything aside from the occasional mysterious letter.

She and Diana managed periodically to make jewelry—pendants and rings and the odd bracelet here and there. And Belle, despite her unusual hours and tendency to disappear for days at a time, ran a quite successful back room where she performed readings and the like.

Diana was occasionally suspicious of the "like," but Belle assured her there was no dark magic or anything dangerous. She was simply helping lost souls find their way, using the talent she'd been given as it was meant to be used.

Belle had a habit of floating around, staying sometimes in Diana's apartment above the shop, sometimes with Bernie in her old room, and sometimes with whatever guy she'd been dating. Currently, that guy was a brawny biker with Celtic-pattern tattoos peeking out the collar of his black leather jacket. Thus far, Diana had only seen brief glimpses of him through the shop windows as he'd swooped in to pick up his passenger without as much as shifting out of gear.

Diana had tried to talk to Belle about the easy way she'd moved from one beau to the next, never finding one worth more than a few weeks of her time and not bothering to be certain her charms left no ill effect, but Belle had only laughed. "Someone's got to make up for the ones you refuse to date."

Diana poured hot water into her special Sunday mug, her infuser filled with the peppermint Bernie had brought her. She made a note to order new infusers, sketching out a possible display that could sit on the sales counter near the register.

The shop didn't sell food, but Diana had to be careful exactly what they stocked and how it was stored. They'd had some trouble with the town council, and even though everything was clear with the state, their local licensing was constantly in probationary status.

She bit down hard, trying not to curse at the woman responsible for it all. Abigail Brown had hated the Coulton sisters since grade school, when Belle had smiled at Abby's first boyfriend and the boy had immediately fallen in love.

Belle swore she'd not done it on purpose, and they'd only been children at the time, but Abby had never forgiven it. It might have been funny that the woman could hold a grudge for so long if said woman hadn't been elected to decide which businesses were up to code—a code that she was responsible for and that somehow seemed to shift depending on what Diana did inside Bad Medicine. So far, they'd had to update the shop signs, relocate the displays three times to comply with alternating emergency egress plans, and cease sales of all candies that were made on the premises. It was beyond frustrating, but short of hexing the fool woman, there wasn't much Diana could do. And they'd promised not to hex anyone again, even when they really deserved it.

She sighed, grateful it was at least a Sunday, when no random inspectors would be stopping by unannounced. Then she remembered she needed to place the order the next day and grabbed her notepad and a fresh pencil to walk once more through the shop.

The front of the store was lit mostly by the sun, natural light filtering through the tall, wide windows on either side of a stained-glass door. There were displays of crystals and jewelry that could be seen from the street, but the more delicate items like candles and plants were only viewable on the antique shelves lining the shop walls. Diana had painstakingly painted each metal tin and glass jar, giving the shop an old-world-cottage feel.

Bernie had decorated the spaces with thin, wiry branches and baubles, tucking greenery in where she could. She cultivated the most gorgeous flowers, and everything from angelica to yarrow was expertly arranged in vining towers between those shelves.

The candies and teas were closer to the sales counter, profiting from impulse buys, and spices and cooking supplies lined the back wall.

A short and highly vetted list of customers had access to the shop's more valuable merchandise: items that could be used for spellcasting and magical arts. Diana didn't think most of the public would even know what to do with those supplies, but that didn't mean she wanted them out where any random customer could touch—and possibly taint—their stock. Besides, with the likes of Abigail Brown out there and the trail of discontent Belle's irresistibility left behind, the Coulton sisters needed to be as careful as possible. Not that anyone was going to point and yell, "Witch!" It was the twenty-first century after all. But still, an ounce of prevention and all that.

A wind picked up outside, blowing a scattering of fall

leaves past the front windows. Diana mentally added *sweep the sidewalk* to her list of chores and started to turn back to checking stock when something red caught her eye. Her stomach tightened, that ill feeling she'd woken with suddenly returned. She laid the notepad and pencil on the sales counter and walked the twenty-six steps to the stained-glass door. Through the delicate pattern of leaves and limbs that made up the glass, she could see the wind had died. It did not stop her dread as she turned the brass lever to unlock the door. She drew it open and glanced down at the welcome mat before the threshold. There in the center, perched precariously over the cursive C, was a black-and-white-dotted feather. A warning.

Change is coming.

Diana stepped out just as the clouds cleared to grant warm sun on her face, and the wind took flight again. It teased her hair gently around her, and what she'd thought was foliage fell through the air once more. Not leaves in autumn hues. Not leaves at all.

Diana was surrounded by a swirling ring of blood red that floated down to settle lightly onto the sidewalk. Her throat thickened, her palms gone sweaty.

Feathers.

Blood red and a portent of love.

A flash of memory from the night before, her sister holding her hand and promising to help her see.

To not be alone.

Diana groaned, dropping her face into her palms.

"Oh, Bernie," she said aloud. "What have you done?"

2

———————

Diana gathered up each and every red feather and placed them gingerly into a woven twine bag. She looped it twice with white string, then folded it into her shoulder bag. She stopped by the sink to splash her face with cool water, and as she patted her skin dry with a hand towel, she watched the droplets in the basin take an unnatural route toward the drain.

Had she any doubt she'd been hexed, the forces of nature were determined to convince her.

She left the shop through the back door, locking both the lever and the deadbolt. She'd placed protections on the property, but there were things inside none of them could risk. She turned around, ready to hop into her car and speed away, and then remembered she'd let Belle use it. She frowned, rummaging around in the shoulder bag for her knit cap, and tugged it down tight over her ears. She put the bag in the wire basket of her mother's old bicycle and climbed aboard to make the six-mile ride to the farmhouse where the sisters had been raised.

Something icy crawled up the skin of Diana's neck, and she jerked to look behind her, but there was nothing there. The shop was on the outskirts of the business district and not exactly bustling on a Sunday afternoon. Nothing stared back at her. There was only the alleyway of gravel and stray weeds and the backs of the adjacent buildings: a successful consignment shop that was only open four days a week and an abandoned hardware store that was never open at all. Diana tightened her grip on the handlebars and headed out of the alley and away from town.

This was how bad things happened, she thought. But that was only on television. This was the real world, and Diana was a witch. It took something serious to be more dangerous than a practitioner of magic.

Like bad hexes, her mind supplied. She winced, pedaling faster, and the old bike bounced up over the rounded edge of the asphalt and onto Dahlia Road.

The way was winding, but traffic was sparse, and she made good time on the blacktop. Before long, the old brick buildings that had once been a part of downtown gave way to trees and split-rail fencing, their white slats separating the road from manicured lawns and heritage farms.

When she finally approached the drive toward the farmhouse, shadows had stretched halfway across the blacktop.

The house sat well off the street, large sugarberry trees obscuring the view from passersby. Diana rode up to the wide porch, tilting the kickstand out to leave the bike beside Bernie's latest half-finished landscaping project. She stepped onto the whitewashed deck boards as she had a thousand times, past the faded rockers and the worn-thin rug. The door opened beneath her hand without lock or key, and Diana tugged the bag tighter onto her shoulder as she came into the foyer. The house was quiet, the only light coming from the windows in the great room. Diana kicked off her shoes and made her way to Bernie's room.

Her sister's door was open, curtains drawn so that the space was divided by swaths of early-evening sun. Two pair of shoes lay haphazardly at the foot of the bed, both Bernie's. Lily, a large silver-furred Siberian Husky, lay snoring on the rug. Diana walked closer.

In the center of the bed was a twisted wad of blankets. "Bernie," she said, none too kindly. She swallowed back the emotions that had been clawing at her all morning. "Bernie."

The blankets did not budge, so Diana moved to the nightstand, picked up a book, and dropped it to the wood-plank floor. It smacked loudly, and there was nothing her sister hated more than an abused book.

Bernie's head shot up through the center of the blanket pile, red hair askew, the entire scene not unlike that of an erupting volcano. "What," Bernie snapped, but her tone was neither a question nor an exclamation.

Diana remembered the throb in her own head hours before. She'd woken to stare into empty space through bleary eyes, with the subconscious knowledge of their mess and a pretty horrid feeling in her gut—and nearly every-where else. She felt just a little bit bad she'd not thought of bringing her sister a tonic. "Bernie," Diana said again.

Bernie's eyes, the same bright blue as the Husky's, met her sister's. "Di," she whispered. "I was just dreaming of you." Her brows drew together. "Are you real? Did I call you here?"

Diana frowned. "You can't dreamwalk, Bernie."

She smiled, apparently relieved. "Right." A massive yawn broke her concentration, then two pale arms came free of the pile to stretch skyward. "Wow," she muttered. "What day is it?"

"Sunday," Diana answered. "Bernie, I need you to focus."

Bernie looked up at Diana as if only then remembering she was there.

Diana resisted the urge to grab her sister out of the blankets and drag her into an ice bath. "I'll make coffee. You have five minutes."

Diana turned to stomp off, nearly jumping out of her skin when she was confronted by Lily, standing silently only inches from her. She was staring at the shoulder bag, which did not include any specially baked doggie treats.

"Oh, Lily," Diana said. "I'm sorry. I'll make you some bacon instead, how's that?"

Lily's face split in a wide grin, her tongue lolling out to the side, and she tore off, back legs skidding beneath her as she slipped on a rug. It spun free of her, but the dog kept going, and Diana knew that when she reached the kitchen there would be a big slobbery mug waiting impatiently by the stove.

Diana was plating up bacon and eggs when Bernie finally came into the kitchen. Bernie had pulled her hair into two cone-shaped buns at the crown of her head, not unlike cat ears, and wore thick-rimmed glasses and a cropped-sleeved black blazer. She looked as if she was doing calculations in her head.

Diana set a plate in front of Bernie's chair and a plate in front of her own. Lily moved to the far end of the table, resting her chin on the tabletop to watch them eat—at a distance she'd been warned to keep. "You already had more than your fair share," Diana told the dog.

Bernie grinned. "Spoiling her again, Auntie Di?"

Diana glared at her sister, taking a bite of bacon before she said, "Eat your breakfast, Bernie. You have work to do."

"Oh," Bernie said. The look she'd had seemed to fade a bit, and she repeated, "Oh." The second sounded less like realization and more like regret.

Diana nodded. "Yes. And now you need to undo it."

Bernie winced. Her head bobbed vigorously in agreement and then slowed. "Oh," she said again.

Diana's fork froze on its way to her mouth. That one had sounded surprised.

Bernie pushed her plate away, put her fingers over her full lips. She looked for an instant as if she might cry.

"Bernie," Diana snapped.

Bernie's mouth fell open, and she shoved away from the table to pace. "Oh," she said. "Oh, no, no, no."

The 'ohs' had progressed to moans, and Diana was on her feet just as fast. When she finally caught hold of a frantic Bernie, her sister closed her eyes and refused to look at her. "What did you do?" Diana asked.

Bernie whimpered. "I don't remember."

The air fell out of the room—or maybe just Diana's lungs.

Bernie's eyes opened, full of remorse. "But I feel like it was bad."

"How bad?"

"When I woke up, my hands smelled like fresh roses. And there was a feather in my shoe."

Diana melted into Bernie's discarded chair. "You don't remember." She stared toward the kitchen windows, darkness falling outside. "You cast a love spell and you don't remember."

Bernie squeaked. "I'll remember," she promised. "Di, I

can figure it out. I promise, I will. Whatever it takes." But she was wringing her hands.

Diana's cell phone rang, buried somewhere in the bag where it hung on a wood-railed chair. Bernie rummaged through it, letting out a cheep when she saw the woven-twine sack, and picked up the cell.

"What's wrong?" the muffled voice said through the speaker.

"Oh," Bernie moaned. "I've done something bad, Belle. Really bad." There was a pause, then Bernie rattled off the afternoon's revelations. "I don't know for sure. I had a lot of dreams, all about Di, and I woke up with rose petals and—yes, I know that, Belle. But I did. I must have. Oh, and now I've forgotten everything and I can't get it undone."

"What's forced into action can never be undone," Belle said through the phone.

Bernie groaned again. "I know, but isn't there—can't I just—I mean I need to do *something* to fix it."

"Okay," Belle said. "Stay calm. Bernie, I need you to think about what you did last night. Walk through it with me."

Bernie was nodding, pacing in front of the counter from sink to stove. "Right, let's do that. Okay, so we were having margaritas and listening to music and—"

Belle said something that cut her sister off.

"I don't remember any of that." She nodded. "Start from the end and work backwards? Well, Diana just woke me up. Yes, I was asleep until this late in the afternoon. Are you the curfew police now?"

"How did you get home?" Belle asked through the speaker.

"Uber?" Bernie said.

Diana's forehead *thunked* against the antique farm table with a groan.

Bernie stopped pacing. "I don't know, Belle. I don't remember any of it. We were just dancing and laughing and then we started talking about men and well, Di looked so sad."

Diana swallowed hard but did not look up.

"I know," Bernie continued. "I'm sorry, Belle. I didn't mean any harm."

Belle's next words came through loud and clear. "What was your intent, Bernadette?"

A chill ran through the room, sudden and sharp. Intent was what mattered in magic, whether you were as powerful as the sisters or not. But Bernie had a talent for making things grow.

Bernie, who had woken with the scent of roses on her hands.

"I don't remember," Bernie whispered. "I don't remember any of it at all."

3

———

In short order, it was decided that Diana would spend the day with Bernie, trying to walk her through possible spells and how they might be counteracted. If they came to no good conclusion by morning, Bernie would run the shop while Belle tried to read whatever ill omens had attached themselves to her. Diana would be babysat. Watched over. Safely under lock and key until they could figure this thing out.

That had been twenty-six hours ago. And now, after a full day of working through every single memory trick they could think of, Diana and Bernie sat sock-footed on the couch with warm mugs of lemongrass tea and candlelight. Bernie could only remember three things about her drunken mid-morning hex: roses, feathers, and the loneliness she'd felt from her sister.

"I'm not lonely," Diana said over the rim of her mug. She resisted the urge to blame the alcohol. Everyone knew drink wasn't that kind of drug—if you said it, no matter how nasty or untrue, it meant those things had been lurking some-where inside you. The alcohol was just an excuse to let it out.

"I know, Di. I think I was caught up in the dancing and song, and I felt... something. Some kind of sadness. Some-thing missing." Bernie snuggled closer to Diana like a puppy who'd been scolded and needed desperately to be forgiven. "I didn't mean to mess things up again."

"You have a good heart, sister. Don't apologize for that."

Bernie lifted her head to glance up at her. "Just for the hexing, then?"

Diana let out a laugh that turned to a sigh. "We'll figure it out. Somehow."

Lily whined from her spot on the floor, and the sisters' gazes snapped to the line of windows. The air looked still, but walnuts were suddenly dropping from the backyard trees. There was a moment of silence, and then every single candle in the room guttered out.

Lily jerked to attention, facing the windows with her ears on point. Diana and Bernie stood, setting their cups down and walking toward the windows without a word. Three large walnut trees stood in a row, their leaves still in the moonlight. On the grass beneath them lay hundreds of walnuts, too early in September for them to have matured.

Bernie cringed. "There goes our walnut harvest."

She and Diana walked down the row of windows toward the door, both knowing whatever foul magic had dropped the walnuts would make them too dangerous to eat. Diana's hand slid over the metal knob, and it felt colder than it had any right to be. She glanced at Bernie then twisted it to open the door.

The air outside was chill, damp, and heavy as if it were going to rain.

Lily whined beside them.

"Storm's coming." Bernie's eyes were on the sky, purple in the dying light. The clouds were dark shadows, moving slowly toward the house.

Diana's voice was a whisper. "You didn't, like, call on someone dangerous, did you?"

Bernie shifted closer, her answering tone low. "I think maybe I was thinking of a dog."

Diana jerked to look at her sister. "A—You did what?"

"Not an actual dog. Just, sort of"—Bernie scratched her forearm—"loyal."

Lily looked up at her owner, head cocked.

Diana pressed her fingers to the bridge of her nose. "So help me, Bernie, if a hairy beast man shows up at my door—"

Bernie laughed. "Oh, come on, Di, none of us was that drunk."

Diana glared at her.

"Well, I know the difference between a man and a wolf. Even if I can't remember anything else."

"Gods, I hope you're right."

"Let's go inside," Bernie said. She gestured toward the impossibly large pile of walnuts. "I can clean this mess up tomorrow."

THE HEX WAS quiet until four in the morning, when Diana woke from a dream of a man trapped inside a fire, his face too shadowed to make out, his muscles corded with tension. He'd needed help. She had wanted to save him. All she could do was douse the flame, cool the air. But a storm was rising, coming for them both, and when she tried to warn the man, she'd been startled from sleep.

Her bare legs were tangled in the sheets, her nightshirt askew. She called a flame to the trio of candles on the bedside table so that she could see her stinging palms. When she raised them to the light, her heart froze in her chest. Dark shadows in the shape of a wolf centered each of her palms. She leapt from the bed, tripping over the mess of sheets, only catching herself with her elbows and forearms. She was afraid to touch anything with her hands.

She stumbled up from the wood floor, scrambling toward the bathroom. She hit the light switch with her elbow, but the shadows were still on her palms. She cursed, running toward the kitchen, only to smack into Bernie in the hall.

"I heard a thump," Bernie explained.

Diana rolled her palms toward her sister.

Bernie grabbed her by the wrists, pulling her to the kitchen and only letting go when Diana was situated squarely in front of the deep apron-front sink. She was humming, just a solid, steady tone that carried no melody. It was something she did when she was scared. Something she did to focus.

Diana might have told her it was okay, but she was too busy trembling, voice caught in her throat. She wanted the rational part of her brain to tell her this wasn't real. That this was something she'd conjured in her dreams after their talk.

She wanted not to think of the man, of the flames.

Bernie was breaking herbs into a mortar, frantically opening cabinets and searching through jars.

Diana stared at the patterns on her hands, at the dark arcs and lines that made up the shape of a howling wolf. Its neck fur was spiked, its eyes closed. It looked as if it was in pain.

Bernie dumped a jug of milk into the sink, remembered too late the stopper, and plunged her hand in to close the drain. She tossed in lavender and sweetgrass and whatever else she'd crumbled into the mortar. She picked up a final jar, pouring blueberry-colored syrup in a triangle over the mixture.

"There." Her bright blue eyes met her sisters', then Bernie gestured toward Diana's hands. "Submerge!"

Diana stuck her open palms into the sink basin, the heat that had blanketed them immediately cooling. Bernie lit a smudge stick, filling the kitchen with cedar smoke. She chanted something in Latin, but Diana could do nothing but bite down the urge to cry.

Her sister felt guilty enough. The last thing she needed was for Diana to melt into a puddle of sobs.

It would be okay. They would figure it out.

Diana was not about to be attacked by a flaming pack of wild wolves, no matter what her frantic paranoia told her.

"Better?" Bernie asked from beside her.

Diana nodded, afraid to take her palms from the sink.

Bernie flicked on the pendant lights over the counter and carefully took hold of Diana's wrist. She drew one hand out of the liquid, turning it to face them.

White and purple rivulets rolled down Diana's arm.

Her palms were clean.

Bernie let out a sigh of relief, patting the skin dry with an embroidered hand towel. They both looked up at the sound of gravel crunching in the drive. It didn't matter that it was just after four in the morning. It would be Belle.

Their sister rushed through the front door, leaving it

open by the sound of things, and down the hallway into the great room where moonlight danced across the floor. She froze when she saw Diana and Bernie standing by the sink, the kitchen smelling of herbs and milk, the air still tingling with magic.

"What happened?"

Bernie let out a small breath. "The spell is closing in. The fates are trying to warn her."

Belle came into the kitchen, dropping her bag onto the table as she plopped into a chair. The bag fell sideways, two candles and a spool of twine rolling out across one of Bernie's hand-stitched placemats. "So nothing you did had a single effect."

Bernie shrugged. "Maybe it slowed it down." She gave an apologetic side glance at Diana. "Maybe it just agitated it."

Diana did not remind them there was only one more day. One day between this dawn and the blood-red loops on her shop calendar.

Belle stood, coming to Diana and wrapping her arms around her shoulders to draw her in for a hug. After a moment, Belle pulled back. It looked like she'd been cutting her own bangs again; they were dark and spiky. Maybe she'd just slept on them wrong. She stared Diana in the face, as if maybe Belle knew her sister was resisting the urge to pat them into place. "I'll make breakfast, and then we can clean up the porch before Bernie goes into town to open the shop."

"The porch?" Di asked.

Belle dropped her arms and scrunched up her nose. "It's covered in live frogs."

Bernie slid down the cabinet fronts to sit on the floor, her pug-patterned pajama bottoms out of place in the magazine-ready kitchen. Lily sidled up to her, nudging Bernie's arm until she finally wrapped it around the dog, defeated. Lily nuzzled Bernie's ear before licking the entirety of her face. Bernie squeezed her eyes tight against the onslaught.

Belle stared down at her. "Why are you dressed like a ten-year-old?"

Bernie kicked her sister's foot with a helpless laugh. "You bought me these for Yule."

Belle bumped elbows with Diana, winked, and then moved to the refrigerator to gather the basket of eggs and a package of bacon. Aside from the occasional licorice stick, Belle didn't eat processed foods, but she knew bacon was Lily's favorite. She did not know the dog had just eaten a half dozen slices the night before. Lily stood at attention, whining as she glanced between Bernie and Belle.

Bernie patted the dog's back with a sigh. "It's okay, girl. Go on."

Lily gave her one more big lick on the cheek and then leapt over her pajama-clad legs, toenails skidding across the floor as she landed beside Belle.

Diana reached to give her sister a hand up. Bernie's eyes glistened, but she managed not to cry. "Thanks, Di." There was a wet slapping sound echoing from the front hall, a reminder Belle had left the front door open—right onto a porch full of frogs. Bernie winced. "I guess I'd better shut that and go get dressed."

4

———

Belle and Diana had finished breakfast by the time Bernie came back into the kitchen. She was wearing a faded sweatshirt, cut-off shorts, and a pair of rubber gardening boots. Her hair was tamed into a ponytail, and between its red frame and her fair skin, her eyes glowed unnaturally blue. She crossed to the sink, grabbing a biscuit from the counter and shoving it into her mouth before she opened the cupboard door to pull out a metal pail and elbow-length dishwashing gloves.

Diana might have laughed if she wasn't aware of the mess they were about to deal with. Belle sighed and pushed her chair away from the table. "Well, Lily, it's your time to shine."

The dog perked up at her name, but Bernie turned a stern eye on her sister. "You can't do that to those poor frogs."

Belle looked up at her. She didn't have to speak; her smile said *watch me.*

Bernie snapped, "Lily Ann Coulton, don't you dare go out that door."

Belle snorted. "When did you give your dog a middle name?" She gave Diana the side-eye that said, *Sounds like somebody's mother.*

"Just now," Bernie said. "I wanted her to actually listen." She narrowed her gaze on Belle. "You're a bad influence on that girl."

Belle crossed her arms. "I'd be careful about pointing fingers today if I were you."

Diana sighed and stood, walking to the foyer to slide on her shoes. As children, the girls would slide sock-footed over the wood plank floor in the fall, and drag in clumps of mud in the spring. Their mother had never complained, she had only smiled, watching them with a fondness that even now made Diana heartsick. She tugged her knit cap over her ears before she opened the front door to the early morning sun.

The porch was coated in frogs. They had been eerily quiet before, but when she took her first step onto the door-mat, a chorus of croaking rumbled through them, echoing horribly off the windows and the siding and seemingly through Diana's bones. She stared at the sea of amphibians, willing her breakfast to stay down.

She felt Bernie beside her. "That's so wrong. It's nowhere near mating season."

"Not for the frogs, anyway," Belle said from behind them.

Bernie turned to swat her sister with a rubber glove, and Lily burst through the door, nearly knocking the three of them over as she went airborne, landing on the porch like a kid off a diving board. Bernie yelped, Belle laughed, and Diana watched in horror as the dog pounced and flailed and trounced the porch full of frogs. A wave cut through the sea of green as frogs leapt from the deck boards to the relative safety of the grass below.

Lily chased after them, sliding across boards that were damp with slimy dew and crashing into the antique rockers and handcrafted tables. Bernie shouted at Lily and cursed at Belle and slid after them both. Diana was frozen for a moment but realized this was quickly becoming the most effective course of action for the whole ordeal. The frogs were nearly gone now, just a few dozen perched on windowsills and scattered across the deck. She leaned against the door frame, watching Belle cackle at Bernie and the dog, the latter of which had lost all semblance of self-control and was maybe the happiest Diana had ever seen her.

Then Bernie slid on the slippery wood, her gardening boot flying skyward as she landed with a thud on her rear. She hiccupped a sound that might have been a laugh or a sob, and Lily abandoned her chase to leap onto Bernie, knocking her all the way flat to do some thorough sniffing and chuffing. Her younger sister only groaned, and with a smile, Diana pushed off the door frame, grabbing a straw broom to shoo away the last few frogs. She returned to the door, passing Belle where she was doubled over wiping tears of laughter from her face, and picked up Bernie's pail to splash the soapy water over the front walk and scrub at the slime.

Lily had lost interest in the chase by then and, having checked that Bernie was safe, was trailing individual frog scents across the yard. Diana leaned the broom against the siding and crossed the porch to give her sister a hand up. When Bernie stood, Diana handed her the empty pail.

"What's this for?"

Diana smiled. "The walnuts."

Bernie's shoulders fell, and Belle added, "Don't dally, sis.

You've got less than two hours to get cleaned up and back to the shop. That order should have gone out yesterday."

Bernie bit down whatever she might have said, because they all knew it was the only punishment she would get for laying the hex in the first place, but it didn't stop her from making a face at Belle on her way past.

Belle leaned on the doorway, massaging her jaw after laughing so hard, then smacked her palms together when she and Diana were alone. "Okay, let's see what sort of ill omens are crawling about you, shall we?"

Diana looked down at the wet boards. "Maybe not out here."

THEY MADE their way into the great room, where the row of windows displayed a disheveled Bernie among a line of walnut trees, their bounty a two-foot-high mound coating the grass.

Belle grabbed a couple of pillows off the sofa and placed them in the center of the open floor, one for her and one for Diana. They sat cross-legged facing each other, forearms resting on knees. Tilly, the crested gecko Belle had inexplicably shown up with one day when they had been kids, waddled across the floor toward the daytime habitat the sisters had set up for her years before.

Belle's breathing slowed, her long lashes closing over dark eyes with each inhale. The atmosphere calmed with her, the air going warm and still, the sound of Bernie shouting as Lily stole walnuts from her bucket seeming far away. Everything about Belle that looked carefree or wild disappeared when she worked, something about the process making her appear almost tame. Diana had known her since she was born, and yet sometimes when Belle read it was as if she was a stranger.

It was easy to become entranced. Diana stared at her sister, followed the lines of her face, the slow movement in her eyes and the stillness everywhere else. Their breathing fell into sync, Diana's worry about what was coming for her falling away.

Belle held her hands open between them, silky red rose petals in the center of each palm. Diana started to wonder where they had come from—if they were Bernie's and part of the spell—but Belle was singing. No one could not listen when their sister sang.

She had the voice of their mother, from long, long ago, but Belle did not care for lullabies and hymns. She preferred modern music, rock and alternative, occasionally a throwback from the seventies. It had made for some awkward readings, but it wasn't about the words when she was working. Witchcraft was all about intent. And Belle, thank the gods, was intent on helping Diana figure out what exactly their little sister had done.

"She's bound you," Belle murmured into her tune. Diana wasn't huge on alternative music, but she was pretty sure that wasn't the original lyric. The rose petals shifted in Belle's palms, and she continued to sing, her voice low and beautiful, the pace slow enough that one might not be able to guess exactly where they'd heard the song. Diana could feel Bernie crying in her room, but it was a happy sort of tears. It was the way she always reacted to Belle's voice. She must have finished gathering the walnuts, which meant far more time had passed than Diana had felt.

"I see the sun," Belle sang, "and then the wind. And with it comes the one there's no way to mend..."

Her words went on, and Diana tried to pick out which were song and which were prophecy. Her arms were heavy, her breathing steady. Then Belle said, "Beware the wolf, and watch for fire, as portents come and build desire."

Glass shattered as two vases fell from the mantel, crashing onto the stone the same instant the candle by the hearth lit. Diana snapped out of her trance, Belle's singing ceased, and they watched as the candle next to it caught, its flame bright, as one by one a line of pillars and tea lights and tapers flared throughout the room, tracing the exterior walls to surround them in a circle of light.

"Oh," Belle said. "This looks... serious."

Diana groaned.

5
———

I t was late afternoon when Bernie called from the shop. Diana hadn't heard the other end of the conversation, because Bernie had dialed Belle. That in itself should have served as warning. They hopped into Diana's car—a late-model sedan that Belle had constantly complained was too practical and not at all *cool*—and made the short trip into town. As Diana pulled around back to park, the door to the shop's private entrance swung open and Bernie stepped outside.

She was bouncing, her palms pressed together as her heels rose and fell at a rapid pace. Belle let out a resigned breath, and she and Diana met their sister at the door. Bernie looked both ways down the alley before ushering them in.

"Don't panic," she started, but fell silent as she apparently realized she had no further advice.

She led them toward the storefront, where the hanging sign in the window was turned to *closed*. At first glance,

Diana thought the dark wood planks of the shop floor were moving. It only took a moment to realize the cause.

Belle crossed her arms. "Caterpillars."

It sounded like an accusation, and Bernie flinched, but Diana couldn't take her eyes off the floor. The black furry bodies had formed a line, trailing over the wood in a shape she could not quite make out. She remembered the black lines formed on her hands, the words Belle had sung in their family home.

She prayed it was not another beast.

They wouldn't find out though, because when Diana moved forward, the caterpillars scattered toward the shop walls. She froze, sensible shoes parked on the plank floor, and watched as their bodies rolled and shuffled under shelves and into cracks. Diana's stomach turned. She did not need an army of caterpillars eating every last herb and flower in the store. She was thinking, *How will we ever get them out?* when Belle leaned in and asked, "So where's Prue?"

Bernie whirled on their sister. "You will not turn her loose to destroy this shop." She came perilously close to pointing a finger but thought better of it. "Don't think I've already forgotten what you did to Lily."

Belle snorted. "That dog had the time of her life and you know it."

"But, really, where is Prue?" Diana asked, glancing around the otherwise intact shop. She knew the cat would not approve of a room full of caterpillars, let alone the magic involved in getting them there.

Bernie shrugged. "She's out."

Diana and Belle turned keen eyes on their sister. "And the order?"

Bernie opened her mouth and then snapped it back shut. The three of them glanced at the clock.

"Bernie," Diana said, exasperated. She walked to the counter, shuffling Bernie's notes and scribbles into a pile over her own neatly organized list. She dug her cell phone out of her bag and dialed before holding it to her ear with a shoulder. She snatched a new, sharp pencil from the cup on the counter. She had fifteen minutes before the order deadline, or hungry caterpillars eating their shop goods would not be the most pressing of their business concerns. Bad Medicine had a slim supply of regular customers, and they could not risk letting any of them down by not getting the supplies in on time. She refused to look at the wall that held the shop calendar, the big red heart that had started all this.

She snapped a finger at Bernie, who was apparently in deep contemplation with Belle. "Get Aunt Sophie's spell book from under the workshop counter. Hers will be the most likely to have a reference to plagues. Find a way to get these things gathered up before they do any damage." Diana had more to say but was interrupted by the customer service agent on the end of the line. "Yes, hi, Margery, this is Diana Coulton of Bad Medicine Books & Herbs. I know this is last-minute, but I need to make an order, please."

Diana tried not to let her annoyance show as Bernie moved past her toward the workshop. Bernie had gone into focus mode, humming that solid note and taking the most direct route as she disappeared into the workshop for the book. By the time she returned, Diana was finishing up the supply order, hoping they'd not missed anything important. "Thank you so much, Margery. I really appreciate you getting this in before—yes, okay—thank—" Her words cut off as she looked up at Belle.

"Hung up on you?"

Diana nodded.

"Can't really blame her. No one likes to work after hours."

Diana rubbed a hand over her face. "Okay, let's do this." She gestured vaguely toward the front of the store, where the caterpillars had disappeared into shelves and foliage.

"Right!" Bernie had Sophie's spell book open on the shop floor, its yellowed pages crackling as she turned toward the section she was after. "Here. Plagues and pestilence." She bit her lip, running a finger over the loopy script. "Hmm... epidemic... blight... contagion..." Her finger smacked against the page triumphantly. "Infestation."

Bernie grinned up at her sisters, who stood with arms crossed staring down at her. She cleared her throat and went back to reading. "Ants, honeybees, fleas..." She looked up again. "There's no caterpillar or moth. Do we go with worms or butterflies?"

"Worms," Belle answered at the same time Diana said, "Butterflies."

Belle gestured toward the book. "What's the spell for each? We'll let that decide."

"Both use cedar and sage, lavender... eggshells for the worms and old lace for butterflies. We'll need a black candle, salt, and a glass bowl for water from the last rainfall."

Diana went to the workshop to gather ingredients while Belle and Bernie moved upstairs to clear a spot to work their spell. Though it would be best to create a circle on the shop floor, they could not risk being exposed by windows or doors that a passerby might peer in.

The apartment was small, but the living area afforded them enough space once the coffee table and ottoman were slid to the outer walls. A bright wood floor with splatters of paint from its previous life as an art studio lay bare, its rugs hung haphazardly over a counter stool. Bernie drew a circle with the salt, Belle placed the lace over the glass bowl, and Diana sprinkled sage and lavender plus a few ingredients of her own over the floor. The black candle was situated in the center, and the three sisters leaned in to gently blow the wick alight.

Their eyes met, each of them aware the trouble this might bring. Once a spell was cast, if they didn't know the means, its undoing was impossible. They could only repair the side effects and hope for the best. They could not try to stop the hex in motion, and so to meddle at all entailed risk. But the shop was more than important to all of them, and hundreds of hungry caterpillars eating it up could not be left unresolved.

They sat, legs crossed and arms outstretched, palm over palm, to create their circle. Eyes closed, faces to the sky, they recited the words Bernie had found in Sophie's book.

A chill ran through the room, lifting the air and rolling it over their skin. They repeated the incantation, voices steady and level, intent clear. Diana tried not to think of the man in her dream, of the lines that had been etched over her palms when she woke. This was about the caterpillars, that was all.

The wind picked up outside, battering loose siding and trim and blowing a stray can down the sidewalk. A car drove by, too fast, the blare of its radio grating and static-filled. Something pricked at Diana's neck, but she resisted the urge to free her hands to swat at it. She thought she heard the croak of frogs outside, but they were too far from the fields for that to be possible. She smelled sage and cedar and then something foul. The thing on her neck bit her, and she cursed, and her mind went to the place that was the fear and darkness of being hexed, of not knowing, of feeling the thing that was to come.

The candle went out.

Belle drew in a sharp breath.

Diana pulled away her hand to see a thin line of blood.

Blood inside a hex was the only thing worse than trying to interfere with one.

It could fuel a spell, make it unpredictable.

Bernie squeaked, and Diana had just enough time to realize she'd smashed a caterpillar—one that belonged to her hex—before the room went dark. Their eyes landed on the window and the sky beyond that had gone from mild to deadly in a heartbeat. Thunder rolled, and then came the horrific thudding of what could only be pelting hail battering their roof.

"What did you do?" Bernie whispered.

It was less of an accusation and more of a presage.

The sky lit up again, pouring rain, pounding hail, and rushing debris past the glass in heavy winds. There was the muffled screech of a cat just outside, then the shopkeeper's bell rang below as the door slammed open into the shop.

"I'll grab Prue," Bernie said.

"I'll get the door," Diana answered.

They all froze as they heard the growl of a bear.

It wasn't a bear, obviously. It couldn't be. It would just be some non-beast *thing* and they would deal with it.

Bernie's hand was in Diana's, and she was squeezing far too tight. "Belle," Bernie hissed, "you go get Prue. I'll stay with Diana."

Belle glared at her. "That growl was your doing." She

pointed a finger at the apartment door. "You made this mess, and you're going to face this with the rest of us."

Diana pressed her hand around Bernie's wrist reassuringly, dragging her fingers from her sister's grip. She nodded, indicating they would go together, and Bernie led the way, painfully slowly, down the steps. She'd gone about a quarter of the way when Belle got tired of waiting and brushed past them, opening the back door to let one angry black cat inside. Prue groused and spat, shaking each paw with a final flick toward Belle. They heard Belle's hissed "I didn't do it," on the third-to-last step, and Diana gave Bernie a final nudge to get her down the short hall.

They could see the front of the shop from the corridor. As the wind blew, a twisted bit of metal bordering the sidewalk outside rubbed against the wrought-iron railing that protected one of the city's trees—the source of the beast noise. Bernie breathed a sigh of relief and rushed toward the door to close the entrance before anything else got soaked with rain and ice.

Diana bent to scratch Prue's head, and Belle latched the back door locks before pulling the shade closed. They looked at each other, relieved, and Diana let out a small, nervous laugh.

That was when they heard the scream.

Bernie's scream was followed shortly by a thud and then, immediately, terrified yips and chirps as she struggled to get words out. Belle and Diana crashed into each other as they ran toward the front room, then skidded to a stop as they took in the scene.

Bernie was standing in the center of the sales floor, hands raised and trembling, head shaking *no, no, no*. The front door stood open, wind and hail ceased. Small puddles of water and ice trailed from the entrance toward Bernie.

At her feet was the body of a man.

Diana gasped. She covered her mouth with a hand, and Bernie whipped around to face them.

Belle spoke calmly, palms out as if she was herding animals. "Bernie, what happened?"

Bernie clasped her fingers together and winced. "He scared me. I—I was rushing to shut the door, and he was just..." She gestured over her shoulder. "He was just there."

Belle waited.

Bernie let out a whimper. "It was instinct. I just..." She

lifted her index finger, guilt apparent, even as she couldn't admit aloud the sin of using it.

Their mother had ingrained that guilt into them when they were young. You did not focus intent. You did not point. It was far too dangerous, even for little girls.

From a grown witch of Bernie's caliber, it could be deadly.

Diana stepped forward, crunching a wayward twig beneath her shoe. At the sound, a hundred moths took flight, coming from under shelves and out of foliage in a swarm of wings and dust. They'd transformed in a matter of hours, and fluttered like a moving cloud through the shop, circling Diana where she stood before shifting and coursing toward the open front door. They swarmed closer together, a dark mass, and then disappeared into the night.

Had it become night already?

Belle followed the path of the moths, swinging wide past Bernie to slam the front door closed and drive home the locks.

She turned, and each of them stared at the man at Bernie's feet.

Diana inched closer and finally, when she felt brave enough, squatted beside the man. He had a handsome face, even relaxed in sleep, but his chin was a little scruffy, and shadows ringed his eyes. She remembered her own fear, even knowing what Bernie had done, and Diana wondered what the spell had wrought on him. He seemed to be wearing a uniform shirt. Diana reached gingerly toward the man's jacket, pinching the edge of it between the tips of two fingers, and flipped it to the side.

She sucked in a breath and stood straight up, nearly

knocking Bernie off balance where she had leaned in to see what Diana might find.

Staring back at them was an embroidered badge that read *Fire Marshal.* Diana groaned, suddenly sick. "No," she whispered. "No, no, no!" Her eyes found Belle, pleading. "This has got to be Abby's doing. She hates us! She sent him to find a reason to shut us down, and now we've…" She gestured helplessly toward the body on the floor. Her arms came in again to wrap around her middle. Her voice had lost its urgency, its venom. "This is going to cost us our business license."

Belle's lips pursed and shifted sideways as she tilted her head. She nudged the body with the toe of her boot. "I don't know. I mean, if she hates you so much, why did she send you a hunky fireman?"

Diana's fisted hands snapped down at her sides. "He's not a fireman!" She took a breath through her teeth. "This isn't a joke. He is a *fire marshal.* As in, enforcing code." She took a step back, hand flying over her mouth. Her sisters were staring at her, so she let her fingers curl slowly into her palm to whisper, "Are caterpillars against code?"

Belle sighed, waving her hands. "Okay, okay, you need to take a break, Di. I can't think with you on this emotional rollercoaster. Come on, let's sit down and get you some tea."

She tried to corral Diana toward the workshop, but Bernie was leaning down, flipping the other side of the man's jacket with the end of a decorative birch twig she'd pulled off the rack. There was a matching patch over the pocket on his other side that read *Miles Wieland.*

Bernie smiled up at them, pleased that she'd discovered his name. "Now we don't have to fish out his wallet."

Diana blinked.

Belle pressed her lips to keep from smiling. "Okay," she said again. "Let's all just take a second to regroup."

Leave it to Belle to have the clear conscience and level head when they'd just killed a man.

"He's not dead," Belle said.

Diana's gaze snapped to hers.

"All I'm saying is that it will all be okay. We have done nothing illegal thus far."

Bernie snorted. "Thus far."

Belle shrugged. "Look, I'm not going to rule anything out. But we need to have a plan, and panic will get us nowhere." She looked at Bernie. "What was your intent?"

"Stop. That was basically all I had time to think."

Belle nodded. "Great. So, nothing permanent."

Bernie bit her lip, as if unsure.

Belle rubbed her face and took hold of Diana's shaking hands. "Tea. Tea first, then a plan."

7

———————

"So, listen," Belle said as she set down her third cup of tea. "I have to cut out of here soon and we still do not have a valid plan."

"Cut out of here?" Diana snapped. "Where are you going that's more pressing than this?"

"I have a thing. I already told you I had a thing."

Diana crossed her arms, leaning back into one of the chairs they'd dragged into the shop to talk while they kept an eye on *the body*, as they'd taken to calling it. "You can't leave."

"We're getting nowhere. Maybe it's best if—" Her sister's glare cut her off. Belle tried again. "We're just wasting breath here. You won't agree to any of my cures."

"Trapping a man in the storeroom and hoping the hex wears off is not a cure."

Belle shrugged. "It's better than anything you've come up with yet."

"Maybe Belle is right," Bernie said. When both women

looked at her, brows raised, she added, "About us getting nowhere. About, maybe, letting the spell run its course."

"Run its course?" Diana scoffed. "Look what it's brought so far. What else is coming, Bernie? How much worse can this thing get?"

Bernie pursed her lips and glanced at the calendar with the loopy red heart.

It had been two days. This was it. In a matter of hours, whatever that permanent marker foretold would be waking and taking shape.

And they had a city official knocked out in the center of their shop floor.

"Let's just put him in the car, drive him downtown, and... you know... let him out," Belle said.

"Let him out?" Diana shot back. "Belle, do you know what criminal charges apply to dumping a body?"

Belle shook her head. "Not really, no. But I'm guessing it's less severe than keeping one in your storeroom."

Bernie nodded. "That's like kidnapping or something. Definitely worse." She stood, tapping her fingers to her lips before curling them anxiously into her palms. "All right, so we take the body out to the car"—she paused, clearly not open to the idea of a strange, spelled man in their only vehicle—"then we shove him into the trunk..."

Diana was so focused on Bernie's fidgeting hands and the possibility of a workable idea that she didn't notice the shuffling sound until it was too late. Until the shadow rose behind her sister.

"Shove him where?"

The voice was deep, scratchy with sleep, and the most terrifying thing Diana had ever heard. Because the voice was coming from the body that had been on the floor.

From Miles Wieland.

Bernie's eyes were bright and wide, filled with the fear that was sending a chill over Diana's own skin. And not because they'd just admitted to a possible felony.

Belle moved slowly, shifting a foot onto the floor as Bernie turned toward the man.

This afforded them each a full view of him as he scanned the shop surrounding him, the unfamiliar shelves and strange flowers, the women perched unsteadily on the edges of their chairs. Discussing where to dump his body.

Diana cringed but could not take her eyes off of him. He was recovered, mostly, and aside from poorly weathering the storm and an apparent lack of sleep, he did not seem in bad shape. Certainly not in mortal danger.

She could not say the same for her family.

"Stay calm," Belle told the man. "You've hit your head, I'm afraid, and there might be a moment or two where you're feeling foggy." She was holding a hand out again in her herding gesture, but now she'd added a bit of the charm that was solely Belle.

Fire Marshal Miles Wieland did not fall for it. He threw up a finger and hissed, "Stay back. Don't even move." The motion seemed practiced, but his gaze was wild.

Belle shrugged. "Look, man, no one is trying to hurt you. You just fell and…"

He was shaking his head, taking a small step back. His eyes hit Bernie. It was plain he remembered what she'd said about shoving him into a trunk.

Belle cleared her throat, tried again. "I'm sure you're confused. You should take a second to—"

"No," he said. The finality of it hurt, but when he reached

for his waist and Diana realized they'd been too foolish to take his cell phone, she drew in a sharp breath.

Miles Wieland looked at Diana then, and in that single instant, every fear inside of her fled. She was seized with a sudden tension, an electric *something* that wanted to draw her nearer. To go to him, to touch him. He did not appear to have the same response. If anything, in that instant, he looked *more* afraid.

He staggered backward for the door, not turning his back on them even when he had a hand on the lever. He fumbled with the lever blindly and then spun as he worked the latch.

"It's locked," Bernie chirped, her intent clear. *Let him go. Get him out of this shop.*

The man glanced over his shoulder, jerking door and lever and making absolutely zero progress. It didn't budge.

"Turn it left," Bernie suggested, while Belle and Diana exchanged a glance.

It was not a broken lock.

It was the hex.

Diana frowned, checking the clock on the wall. It hadn't merely *seemed* like a long time since they'd been watching the body on the floor. The hands of the clock had stopped ticking. The spell was working its magic not just on the poor man wrestling with their shop door; it had tricked the sisters.

It had made them think they had time. A chance to beat it.

She would have to remember that, the way it was so easy to fall into its scheme.

Belle moved, and Diana's gaze shot back to the situation at hand. The man—Miles—had turned on them, his accusing finger aimed again.

He thought they had trapped him. Locked him inside.

It was going to be a long night.

"Let me go," he demanded. "Whatever you're doing—" But his words cut off, because he apparently couldn't quite decide what the women intended. They'd been discussing dumping his body, after all.

"Okay," Belle said. "Easy there, big guy. Let's just take a second and recap." She motioned toward the offending door. "We were just here, waiting out the storm, minding our own business. *You* were the one who broke into *our* shop after hours and, I might add, without so much as a howdy-do." She crossed her arms and managed to somehow look entirely put out and wrongly done. "I have a mind to call the police *on you.*"

Bernie's eyes were wide, but she seemed to be trying her best to play along. "Yes, sir. What, exactly, is your intent?"

The man's gaze flicked between them, evidently seeing through their bluff. Besides, they'd not bothered to call the entire time he'd been unconscious. Obviously, he believed they were hiding something. The thought was plain on his face: *These women have bad intentions.*

Diana sighed. Oh, if he only knew the half of it.

8

———

iles Wieland was no pushover. He was not going to
be foiled by three women or a locked door. He
grabbed a tall, wrought-iron candelabrum from the shelf
and wielded it like a bat—trying his best to ignore the delicate hand drawn tag swinging from it by a ribbon. He knew
there would be another door, some other form of exit, but it
appeared he'd have to pass through his attackers to find it.
Past the woman.

"Stay where you are." He let his tone ring clear: he had a
weapon and he would not hesitate to use it.

The raven-haired woman bit her lip in a smile.

Miles did not see anything whatsoever to laugh about.

He moved forward, carefully avoiding the wide brown
eyes of the brunette. He would not look at her. He would not
think about how he'd seen her before. She could not have
been in his dreams—he'd never even met her. It was just a
coincidence, someone who looked exceptionally similar to
what was unquestionably only a figment of his imagination.

He would not let himself be fooled by a trick of the light or a knock on his head.

There was no way it could be real.

The raven-haired woman eyed the brunette and shrugged. "Okay," she said, stepping to the side to allow Miles past. "Go on."

His gaze narrowed on her, but she only raised a hand to gesture him toward the back. The redhead bounced on her feet, agitated and anxious, and he wasn't sure if she really, really wanted him to leave or if she was deciding how to stop him.

Miles was convinced she'd hit him over the skull. He just couldn't remember exactly how.

He would worry about that later. He eased past the women, the air about them smelling something like smoke and pine. It was too familiar, but he refused to let his thoughts linger on that either.

There were a register counter and a few shelves and, between and beyond them, an opening to what looked like a narrow corridor. He was either trapping himself in a hallway or finding his way out. He glanced over his shoulder at the women and decided the hallway it was. He rushed forward, afraid if he did not, he would again be tempted to find her. To follow his urge to search out the brunette, to allow himself to believe.

When he turned back around, Miles Wieland—seasoned firefighter and trained marshal—screamed like a little girl.

The shadowy mass came out of nowhere, leaping at his face and bounding off his makeshift weapon. The metal candelabrum clanged to the floor and the beast—a thick black cat—hissed, its short fur going spiky as Miles fell backward, stumbling into the wall before sliding the rest of the way to the floor.

"Prue!" someone shouted behind him, and suddenly the women were running, doing nothing to settle the chaos that was a tangle of Miles and candelabrum and angry cat.

The brunette stood over him, her face flushed and hair wild, and Miles had the sudden sickening realization that he'd landed on his rear in front of an audience. So much for giving the appearance of having the upper hand.

The woman sighed, leaning forward to reach for the cat. "I'm so sorry," she told Miles. "I don't know what's gotten into her."

For a moment, Miles was able to avoid staring at the brunette and to see the look exchanged between the other two. But when she came closer, a strange sort of buzzing ran through him, and Miles could look nowhere but into the eyes of this woman he could swear he knew.

"You don't," Miles said.

The woman stopped, leaned over and cradling the beast she'd gathered to her chest. "What?"

He shook his head. "I don't... I mean, I have to go."

She looked sad for some reason. Not that he was leaving or that he wanted to but something else. Like she was sad *for* him. Sorry for him, even.

He felt his head tilt as he stared at her. He couldn't seem to stop, even though he should have been scrambling toward the door. He took in her warm eyes, her soft hair, the line of her jaw. Skin he could nearly remember touching.

"Is it you?" He heard his words but hadn't meant them to escape.

The brunette smiled, something that seemed involuntary, automatic. It was radiant.

Behind her, the raven-haired woman said, "Wow. He is so screwed."

"Di," the redhead supplied helpfully. "Her name is Diana."

The brunette turned to glare at the other women.

Miles used the chance to escape despite the odd pain in his chest. He pressed backward, scooting away and climbing to his feet without letting them out of his sight. The cat watched him from the woman's arms.

Diana.

Miles turned, ignoring the chill running over his skin, and made the last few steps to the door. He grabbed the handle, yanked, and felt himself flush red when it did not move. He fumbled with the lock, turning it every possible way, and still, the door would not budge.

He closed his eyes and drew in a steadying breath.

He felt the women behind him, silent and still, watching.

He turned the lock again, saw it clear the door frame.

Pulled the lever hard.

Breathed again.

Miles, he thought, *just pull the damn thing open.*

His palm was slick against the lever, but he lifted, twisted, tried every trick he'd ever learned to unstick and open a door. He glanced at the hinges, clean and rust free, scanned the frame for blocking or a hidden stop or anything that could be keeping him from dislodging it. There was nothing, no way that both exits could have been sealed with these women inside. It had to be him. He had to be losing his mind.

His forehead *thunked* against the slab. He straightened. Cleared his throat.

Turned to face the women.

They stood near the entrance to the hallway, the raven-haired woman and the redhead wedged slightly behind the brunette and her cat. He had the strangest feeling they were watching to see how his battle with the door would play out. The redhead bit her lip.

"Maybe try"—her index finger came up to wiggle in the air—"moving it the other way?"

The raven-headed woman swallowed a snort.

"The door has been in working order," the brunette assured him, her voice too loud, too formal. "The entire property is up to code. And if there is—if you do find a new issue, the law allows me to repair it before business hours and—"

The brunette's words cut off.

Miles realized why. She had thought he was there to inspect the building. To shut down her business. His expression must have told her otherwise. Had that been why they'd decided to knock him out and drag his body to their car? Good lord, what were they hiding here that was worth felony kidnapping?

He took a step toward them.

They all stepped back.

"Eeep," said the redhead. She glanced at the brunette. The one she'd named Diana.

"Well," the raven-haired woman said from beside them. "I guess that answers that." She glanced at her watch, a thin black band tangled within layers of string. "I'd love to stay and help you explain this to him, Di, but I've got an important engagement." She patted the brunette on her shoulder. "Bernie will help you sort it out." The raven-haired woman smirked at Miles while she spoke to the other women. "Clearly you're safe. He's all but forgotten his candle holder."

Then she turned, strolled to the front door with nary a backwards glance back, and opened it. Without so much as a twitch.

Miles stared.

The redhead shrugged and grinned sheepishly.

The brunette looked worried.

Miles pushed through them, striding purposefully toward the store's entrance.

"Um," the redhead started. She faltered, as if unable to decide what to say.

"I'm not sure you should do that," the brunette called to his back.

It was too late. He was leaving.

He grabbed the lever, yanked open the door, and stepped into the darkness.

He'd not even had the chance to let his eyes adjust before lightning cracked at his feet.

When her unwitting victim finally woke, it was late the next day. Diana couldn't say she wasn't grateful, because she'd needed rest and time to think. But part of her felt guilty about the hex knocking him out two times in a single night. She couldn't imagine he deserved what he would be going through, even though she had no idea what the hex had planned.

She and Bernie had dragged Miles up the stairs to Diana's apartment, depositing him on the sofa centering her living room wall. Even as he'd been asleep, Diana had fought the strange electric urge to keep her eyes on him, to be near him, to touch his skin. The sisters had hurriedly cleaned up the remnants of their spellcasting, and Bernie had promised to read through Aunt Sophie's spell book during every break she got between the duties of the shop.

Because regardless of the rogue magic that had invaded their lives, it was a Wednesday, and below her apartment, the shop was open.

Diana resisted the urge to smack a palm over her face, instead grinning reassuringly toward the man who'd just awoken on her couch.

His eyes widened.

Okay, she told herself, *maybe that was more* deranged *and less* reassuring. She cleared her throat and leaned forward to hand him a glass of water. "You bumped your head again, I'm afraid. I think you should stay lying down and try to take it easy for a bit."

Miles didn't glance around the apartment, didn't bolt for the door. He only stared at her.

She tried to pretend it wasn't disconcerting. That it didn't send an answering buzz of magic through her. "Miles, will" —she glanced around the room herself, trying not to come off as overly eager for his answers—"will someone be looking for you? I mean, is there anyone you'd like me to call?"

He moved to sit up, and Diana swiftly crossed from her chair to prevent him from doing so. It put them too close, put him within touching distance. She managed to resist.

"I think you should rest for a while," she said. They couldn't let him leave, not with the hex working so hard against him. He could be injured, or—worse—someone might see.

Might catch on to the magic behind it.

"I don't—" He looked at the floor by his feet then back at Diana, apparently bewildered. "I was just walking down the street. I can't even remember where I was going—only that I really needed to be there." The corners of his eyes crinkled as he recalled how he'd ended up in their shop, and Diana tried not to notice how those eyes were a brown she was sure she'd seen before. He shook his head. "The storm came out of nowhere."

He sat silent for a breath, and Diana watched nervously for the moment he remembered the rest.

Belle had coached her through what to say. She was ready.

Miles bolted to his feet and pointed a finger at Diana. "You—you were going to stuff me in your trunk."

Diana managed a startled laugh, though her posture was far too still. She knew she should have lurched back at his sudden movement. "You're kidding," she said. "Oh, Miles, no. We were just trying to figure out how to get you to the car. To take you to the hospital. Bernie, she was only saying we may have to move some of my supplies to the trunk. You know, just so we'd have room." She swallowed. Breathed. Looked into his eyes. "And then you got up, and honestly, you seemed fine. Aside from a bit of wild candlestick-wielding, of course, but we forgave you that, given how you'd been through a fall and all." She shook her head, as if regretful. "I'm afraid you overdid it though. We shouldn't have let you trot around like that so soon. Next thing we knew, you were right back on the floor."

His gaze narrowed on her.

She sighed. "I wish we could have gotten you to a doctor, just to be sure, but the storm was something terrible. So we put you up here to rest. Above the shop."

Diana held her breath. If this didn't work, they were going to have major problems.

"I don't know what you think you're trying to pull here," he started, but then he just shook his head as if fighting his own emotions.

Diana knew the feeling.

"I understand," she told him. "I can't imagine waking up in a strange place like you did, but Miles, I understand. You're welcome to leave." She let her sincerity show in her face. "We only—I wanted to make sure you were safe."

He wet his lip, ran a palm over the hip of his jeans. Diana's apartment was especially calming in the daylight. Diana normally had a bit of that talent as well, but she wasn't certain how efficiently her charms were working on Miles, not with the hex roiling through him. "I'm sorry," he told her. "I must have overreacted."

Diana had the feeling Miles Wieland did not normally overreact. She knew for certain he'd not overreacted the past night. If anything, he'd allowed them too much leeway.

If they'd been any other witches, it would have been too late.

"That's entirely reasonable, given the circumstances." She offered him a reassuring smile. "Can I make you some coffee? Or a hot tea?"

"Coffee, extra sugar." His answer was almost automatic, and Diana couldn't help but grin.

Fire Marshal Miles had a sweet tooth.

She found that unreasonably cute.

Diana ducked her head as she moved to get them coffee, ashamed she'd let a fool curse trick this perfectly sensible man into her home and mortified she was even remotely enjoying it.

Belle was never going to let her live this down.

MILES FINISHED his coffee in near silence. Diana's fingers were wrapped around her own mug like it was the only thing keeping her afloat. She'd wracked her brain with excuses to keep him there, and she'd fought her conscience on letting him leave. There was no good answer, aside from protecting him as best she could while the curse ran its course.

And even that held more than a few serious dangers for them both.

He finally looked up at her, his eyes clear as they sat on her pale, deep-cushioned couch. "I guess I should go now." He set his mug on the side table. "Thank you for the..." Miles gestured toward the coffee cup so vaguely as to encompass the entire room and all that had transpired.

Diana set her mug down as well, nodding with resolve. She would do it. She would let this man leave, come what might. She would not hold him here against his will.

She walked him toward the apartment door and stood aside so he could make his way down the stairs. He was tall and broad, and so near that the tingle of the curse felt pleasant instead of urgent. "It was nice to meet you, Miles Wieland."

He smiled perfunctorily and walked past her and into the stairwell. He made it to step three before he turned around. "What—how do you know my last name?"

Diana felt her face pale, unable to gain composure enough to tell him that it been printed on his shirt. She watched in horror at what she knew was coming, but could only throw her hand forward in an attempt to stop him from backing down the steps. Her voice was trapped in her throat.

She couldn't warn him.

Prue screeched as his boot hit her side, and Diana was helpless as Miles tried to correct, misstepped, and tumbled backward.

Diana's hissed *"Prue!"* came out like a curse, and she was rushing after the man.

She made it to the landing in time to see him collide with Bernie at the foot of the stairs, where she'd apparently run to find the cause of the commotion, giant basin in hand. He toppled her, sending the basin crashing spectacularly into the opposite wall.

They lay there, apparently shell-shocked for a moment, before the liquid that had splashed from the basin started to burn Miles's skin.

He shot up, hissing and tearing his shirt free, while Bernie stared up at him from her spot on the floor—not simply because he was ripping off his clothes, Diana thought, but also—somehow—every drop of what had spilled had ended up solely on Miles, soaking through jacket and shirt.

Bernie glanced sheepishly at Diana, who now stood with her hand covering her mouth.

She hadn't quite decided if she was holding in a laugh or a sob.

"Bernie," she said, "what is that?"

Bernie cringed. "He needs to wash it off. Use lavender oil and catmint, and that special soap I hid under your sink."

Diana nodded, holding her hand out for Miles while Bernie stood and urged him to follow. The shop door dinged. Bernie glanced over her shoulder then back at Diana, who gave her a nod that she had it handled. She could wash off a shirtless man the hex had attacked, surely she could manage that.

Diana rushed up the stairs with Miles, took a detour to the cupboard under the sink, then led him to the door of her tiny bathroom. "Leave that here," she said, gesturing toward his shirt. "I'll get some gloves on and clean it up." She shoved the bottles at him. "Soap first, then follow with the lavender oil and catmint." She pointed to a tall white cabinet beside the shower. "Towels are in there, and I've got a robe on the back of the door."

He looked as if he wanted to say something, but clearly the burning took precedence.

"Hurry," she ordered, shooing him in.

He tossed the drenched shirt on the floor by her feet as instructed, and Diana couldn't seem to stop herself from glancing up at him. He turned, hastily grabbing for the door to press it shut.

Diana froze, holding her breath to stall a sudden intake of breath.

The door clicked shut in front of her, but she could only stare on in dull shock.

On Miles's muscled back, at the flat of his shoulder, had been an inked design.

Howling.

Spike-necked.

Closed eyes.

The wolf.

Her palms instinctively curled into fists at the remembered pattern.

This man was the target of Bernie's hex.

Its quarry.

She was sure of it in a way she could no longer deny. This poor man was prey, no matter what she did. The hex would not let him go until... until what? What had her drunken sister plotted in the dawn light to release them from this spell? A bond? A sacrifice? True love's kiss?

A helpless, hysterical laugh escaped Diana, and the door opened a crack.

Miles peered down at her.

She cleared her throat. "Just, uh, getting the shirt."

He watched her for one instant longer before the door clicked shut again.

Diana slid onto her bottom, sitting as she stared blankly across the room. She was so screwed.

10

Diana listened to the cascade of the shower on the other side of her bathroom door, only snapping back to the issues at hand when she finally heard the squeak of the tap that brought the water's cease. She stood, gingerly picking up Miles's shirt between two fingers by its collar. She carried it to the kitchen, tossed it into the sink, and dumped a mix of Bernie's homemade detergent over the top of it. She ran cold water over that, and when it looked as if the water ran mostly clean, she reached in to scrub and wash and then wring it dry. She hadn't truly needed gloves, but she couldn't tell Miles that.

Prue leapt onto the counter, staring down her nose at the mess.

"Don't say it," she told the cat, though the cat had never actually spoken her criticisms aloud. She didn't need to; Diana could read it on the feline face.

Diana snapped the shirt into shape, draping it over a chair back and straightening the collar and sleeves. She jumped when she turned and saw the figure watching her work.

"Oh," was all she managed, hand flying to her bare neck.

Miles stood shirtless and barefoot before her in nothing but a pair of well-worn jeans. He held the lavender oil in one hand apologetically, a white cotton towel in the other. She was struck by the sight of him, sculpted muscle from his broad chest all the way down, into the waist of his low-slung jeans. She flushed hot as her gaze trailed over his chiseled abdomen, then remembered herself, and that he was waiting for help with the oil. She cleared her throat.

"I'm so sorry," she told Miles, brushing an errant lock of hair from her face. "I didn't even think about that. Here, let me."

She walked toward him, taking the bottle from his hands without a second thought until the tingle hit, the strange desire to touch him more.

The urging of the magic.

Miles studied her eyes, expression unfathomable. She was a stranger, and yet, they'd been forced together since the curse had struck. It had managed to have him half-dressed in her apartment with the promise of her fingers on his skin. She swallowed hard and gestured for him to spin around.

His back was red, but, fortunately, not blistered. The wolf tattoo stared down at her accusingly.

Diana's gift gave her the power to heal, but it was a complicated thing. The process could be painful—for both her and the recipient—and she'd no desire to try to explain an unnaturally speedy recovery to someone who was already suspicious of her. It was not as if his life was in danger from the injury. She dripped oil onto her fingertips before pressing them gently against his back. He tensed, but she couldn't be sure if it was that his flesh was tender or the unbearable feel of her skin on his. Of the touch that was fulfilling the desire to bring them closer. She pressed her eyes closed, knowing that touch must have been how Bernie had tied them.

What she was doing would strengthen the hex.

She breathed deeply, all too aware there was nothing to be done for it. The storms had proven that. The doors, the cat in his path. Nothing would stop it, until Bernie's intent was sated.

The hex slid over Diana's skin and swam between them. At her sigh, Miles glanced over his shoulder. She ducked into her work and away from his appraisal, applying the oil to every bit of exposed skin. Miles held incredibly still, though she sensed he meant to speak a half dozen times.

"What was that?" he finally asked of the mixture he'd been doused in when he'd crashed into Bernie.

"Cleaning solution," she lied. "Bernie—that's my sister who you... met... downstairs—she uses it to scour the basins. It doesn't look too serious; you should be fine in a couple of hours." If his tension was any indication, the oil had already eased any burning he felt.

"Your sister," he said.

"Yes. And the other is Belle, with the black hair and the gentle manners."

His back shifted as he covered a snort at Belle's gentleness. "And you all work here in this shop?"

"Bad Medicine Books & Herbs. We're going on our third year." As long as they didn't let the county fire marshal decide their shop was possessed, anyway.

Diana's fingers slid over his broad back, and she made

herself draw them away, even as the tingle lingered on her palms. *Touch him*, the curse whispered. *Tie to him.*

Miles turned to face her, where they stood for an uncomfortably long moment. She wondered if it was whispering to him too. Or if it was more of a scream.

Miles's gaze fell to her lips, and she realized she'd let her mouth come open—with nothing to say. She grabbed the towel he was holding. "Let me get this." She jerked it free before he let go his grip, and he stared at her as she brushed past him.

Diana didn't look back, only tossing the towel into a basket with some other things as if she was going to do laundry right then, for fate's sake.

Miles cleared his throat behind her, where he'd moved near the kitchen counter. Prue was posted on the opposite end of that counter, eyes on this strange intruder. As if the beast had not managed to tangle with him twice as it was.

"I need to make a call," Miles started.

Diana interrupted him, dropping the basket to walk toward the door where she kept her purse. "Oh, you need a ride. I'm sorry, I should have offered. Just let me get my keys and—"

He held up a hand as she crossed the space. Diana froze.

"That would be great. Thank you. But I'm afraid my cell phone's dead, and I've missed a meeting. Just a quick call first, if you don't mind."

"Of course," she said, hating the way her voice went weak and airy. The curse was not going to like this. She couldn't both make it happy and let him leave. But if she went with him... maybe...

She remembered Miles was waiting for her and grabbed her phone from her bag. If the fates were kind,

Belle would not have plastered another inappropriate image as her background screen while she'd been distracted. Diana had yet to figure out how to remove them on her own, so whatever it was, she wouldn't have time to hide it.

She walked around where Prue was posted to hand the phone to Miles.

"Thanks," he said, lifting it toward her in what she took as an indication he intended to make the call in private.

Right, then. She put her head down, bent for the basket she'd been fooling with, and left him to it while she carried the clothes downstairs to the small utility room.

She could feel the curse pushing her back, trying to get her again up the stairs. To Miles.

Its target.

She would not listen.

She'd no more than opened the lid to the washer before Bernie was beside her. "What are you doing?" her sister hissed.

Diana shook her head, refusing to acknowledge the bright red rose petals inside the tub. She closed the lid on the machine. "I don't know. Laundry, I guess?"

Bernie grabbed Diana's shoulders to force her to meet her gaze. "You left him alone in your apartment?"

"Yes, why wouldn't I?" Her mouth fell open when she realized all the reasons not to—not because of the curse but because of all the evidence of magic.

This was so much harder than she had imagined it would be. Diana Coulton didn't let outsiders into her life. She liked being alone, being responsible for things within her control. She liked schedules and order. And she was *not* a good liar.

"Go," Bernie whispered. She shooed Diana away and took hold of the laundry basket. "I'll handle this."

Diana frowned, and Bernie leaned in to give her a quick hug.

"You can do this," Bernie whispered.

Diana closed her eyes against any tears that might come, took a deep breath, and leaned back to nod at Bernie. By the time she made it to the stairs, her sister's words had fortified her courage. She *could* do this. She would.

She had no other choice.

Her foot touched the stairs silently, and she realized she was not wearing shoes. It felt strangely bare, exposed. There was a man in her apartment, half-dressed and tied to her by rogue magic. She took another step, and the muffled sound of Miles's voice came clearer. She hesitated, wanting to give him his privacy but not wanting to leave him alone.

And then his words cut through.

"...yes, off of Dahlia... are you sure? Do the records show anything else? Previous owners, maybe?"

Diana held utterly still, her head tilting toward the open apartment door.

He was talking about Bad Medicine. Checking her records.

She had a half second of panic, wondering what those records might expose, and then another of outrage—until she remembered Bernie bringing up the idea of going through his wallet. He was just checking up on her. There was no harm in that, was there?

She couldn't be sure. But the idea of exposing her secrets —of the potential it had to harm her sisters—became more untenable with every beat of her heart.

She took another step, and then she was practically running.

She rounded the corner loudly, coming into the room the way her sister might have done, ridiculously suddenly. Miles had been caught, and there was no hiding it.

He didn't try.

"Thanks, Chip. No worries, I'll catch you later." Miles's voice was calm, casual, and he only nodded toward Diana as he ended the call. A *thanks for letting me use your phone* gesture, she thought.

She crossed her arms, somehow more annoyed by his air of unconcern. "Everything good?"

"Yeah," he said, his tone smooth, as if he'd not just rifled through her personal information while using her own borrowed cellphone. "Ready for that ride now, I think."

Diana smiled thinly. "Yeah," she echoed.

She seemed to be ready to let him face the curse after all.

11

———

By the time they'd donned shoes and Miles had buttoned up his still-damp shirt, Diana had all but forgotten Miles's battle with the shop doors. He, apparently, had not. He stood before the back door of Bad Medicine, watching it with a distrustful eye.

Bernie was in front with a customer, so Diana wanted to get out of the shop without bringing her sister's advice and/or panic attack about the excursion into that customer's view. "Just open the door, Miles," she said.

He narrowed his gaze on her but reached for the lever.

He looked more than a little surprised when it opened with ease.

Take that, her inner voice crowed—to both the man and his potential code violation. She strolled past him toward the car, only remembering the lie about the backseat being full when Miles leaned over to peer in the window. She put the key in the ignition, giving him the choice to either get in or walk home.

85

He took the hint, opening the door and sliding into her passenger seat without a word.

So far, so good, Diana thought, shifting the car into reverse.

Miles glanced around as they drove, probably confused as to why such a horrible string of storms had left so little damage. She resisted the urge to fill the silence with chatter. She would only talk about her sisters and that would only invite more danger. She turned right onto the street in front of the shop, where she might normally head left for their family home, before remembering to go through the charade of asking where he lived. She glanced at him but forgot how to speak entirely when she saw the way he was watching her.

He turned quickly away as if shaking himself. Diana's eyes went back to the road and the stoplight at their intersection was suddenly red. She slammed on the brakes, bit down on a curse, and held her breath when the radio played without either of them touching the dial.

Miles stared at the radio centering the dash and then at Diana, and this time she could tell it was not with that sort of ... *awe* he'd had before. This was something else. The fear had returned, not like he was scared of her but like he knew something was wrong.

As if this whole affair was a fever dream.

Or maybe he'd been drugged.

"Silly thing," Diana said. She was shooting for offhand, but her voice came too loud over the music. "Every time it gets jostled, it goes on and off."

The radio sang about being held spellbound in the night, about dancing shadows and firelight. Diana glared out the window at the unseeable naught that was the curse, but it did not seem to care. The light stayed red. The radio carried on with its *woohoo*-ing about a witchy woman. Miles kept his eyes on the remarkably calm weather.

Diana had been terrified of what the curse might bring and then annoyed at its utter inconvenience and downright disregard for her schedule, but somehow she had let it start to settle in her. She had accepted that she would have to live through it—or at least try. But suddenly, in that flat resignation and the stillness of a single stoplight, she became painfully aware of being alone in her very tiny, very uncool sedan with a very large man.

She glanced at him in her peripheral vision, the way his hands perched on his jeans, his legs uncomfortably wedged between seat and dash. She tried not to think about those hands. His legs. The way it had felt to touch his skin. About the lines of his muscled torso and the way she'd flushed with heat despite herself.

This man was a stranger.

Even the curse should have known her better than that.

Miles turned to look at her, and their eyes caught. She flushed, maybe from stealing glances, maybe something else. Miles's gaze stayed on her. Her skin tingled. She thought maybe the car was a thousand degrees.

The truck behind them honked.

She jerked, glancing in the rearview mirror before seeing the light had not actually changed. She guessed they were just tired of waiting.

She guessed she was too.

Diana pressed the accelerator and drove through the intersection, heedless of the traffic laws. Her passenger didn't argue, but she wasn't certain he'd even noticed the light. Sparks still lingered in the air around them. She knew what she was experiencing was nearly unbearable, but she couldn't know what the magic was doing to him.

"Are you feeling okay?" she offered. Just to check. To be sure of at least that much.

He shook his head. Not a *no* but shaking off something, the same gesture she'd seen him use repeatedly since the hex took effect. "Yeah," he said anyway. "I'm sure it'll be fine."

She nodded and turned left onto Main Street. "I'll leave you some sage and lemon balm tea. It should help headaches or... confusion. I'm sure I've got some in my bag." She glanced over her shoulder to verify she'd dropped it in its place, and Miles grabbed the wheel.

The car jerked, bounced over the sidewalk, steering wheel juddering beneath her palms as they headed off the side of the road. Diana somehow managed to slam on the brakes before hitting a tree. Chest heaving in sharp breaths, she stared at Miles where he leaned across her, hand still frozen to the wheel.

His eyes were huge, searching the space around them.

She was afraid to ask, but the words came in a whisper. "What was that?" They were so close. She was sure he could feel the heat of the words on his skin.

He shook his head again. "I don't know. A—a dog, I think."

He did not sound confident. His brow drew down, gaze coming back to hers.

They were inches from each other. His brown eyes were lighter in the afternoon sun, deep with flecks of black and gold. They were kind and intelligent and seemed to speak of protectiveness, carefulness. These were the things Diana could read in a man's eyes. There were so many other things she could not.

Her lips tingled with that spark of magic, with the urging of the curse.

It wanted her to move closer to him.

It wanted them entwined.

"Not that easy," she murmured to it.

Miles seemed somewhere between taken aback and confused. Then he seemed to realize he was braced in Diana's space, practically pressed up against her. The confusion remained, but his other emotions became a sort of apology. He probably assumed the words had been meant for him.

"Thank you," she hurried to say. She gestured wildly, flustered. "For the—for saving my car."

He looked out the window again, as if only then remembering the missing beast. "Should I check to see if anything was hurt?"

"No," she snapped. Then, sheepishly, she added, "I'm sure it's fine. No sense in getting out there where there might be a rabid dog." Her laugh held an edge of hysteria. "I'm sure nothing's hurt. We would have heard it if I'd torn anything up under the car."

Truly, that was the least of their problems.

He leaned back into his seat and adjusted the shoulder belt as he slipped it across his chest.

"Okay," Diana said aloud to the car and the curse. "Let's try this again."

She backed carefully onto the road then slipped the car into drive, thinking, *Everything is fine. The hex won't kill us. It's not as drastic as that. We just have to appease Bernie's intent.*

"Diana," Miles said.

She nearly jumped out of her skin, despite his voice being quiet and calm. She answered, "Hmm?"

"Did I tell you where I lived?"

Her breath escaped. "You said over by Landry Park, didn't you?" It was cruel to make him think he'd forgotten, that he'd really bumped his head that hard. But Diana wasn't her sister. She could not lie so easily. She had to work with what she had. "I'm sorry—am I going the wrong way?"

"No," he said. "I just... I didn't remember telling you."

She smiled. "You didn't. Only the whereabouts. So, where to from here?"

He gestured toward the next intersection. "Right on Hawthorne, three blocks to the Eaton Estates. There's a stone gateway there, can't miss it."

His voice was kind enough but a little absent. He was worried about his head, probably. It wasn't the least of what he'd faced, she supposed.

"Got it." She smiled. Kindness would not kill her.

None of this was his fault.

It was not as if *he* was the one forcing her to think steamy thoughts about a stranger every time she looked at him, after all. That was the curse.

Clearly.

She slowed to turn onto the Eaton Estates drive, unlined pavement that led to a half-dozen newly built homes. It was a pretty neighborhood, helped along by well-placed trees and excellent landscaping. Diana thought Bernie would like it, too. Miles directed her through the winding drives, and his mood seemed to improve. He was nearly home. She was not some crazed woman trying to stuff him in her trunk. She was just a nice lady giving him a ride after a strange string of unfortunate accidents.

It would all be fine.

"Thanks again for doing this," he told her. "I'm afraid you were right. I must have hit my head a bit too hard."

"No problem," she answered. "You should probably take it easy for a few days, just to be safe."

He nodded. "I'm glad you found me, Diana Coulton. Who knows what sort of trouble I'd be in otherwise."

She let out a helpless laugh. "You're welcome to come back anytime," she offered. "To the shop, I mean." Then, because she could never seem to shut her fool mouth around a nice-looking man, she added, "During normal business hours, of course."

Miles laughed. It was deep and rich and set the butter-flies inside her belly aflutter. "Of course," he echoed. "It's just around this last corner," he started, but his words trailed off as they rounded the line of evergreens that gave way to the property at the end of the subdivision.

The yard was awash with white box vans and men in navy-blue uniforms with clipboards and masks. And the house—though she could only assume it was a house—was covered in a massive yellow-striped tarp.

Diana's voice was a quiet tremor. "Is that yours?"

Miles had paled, his expression blank. He reached for the door handle before Diana had even pulled to a stop. She helped him as soon as she reached the curb, as he could only fumble with his seat belt buckle—not able to look away from the circus that was his home in order to see the latch.

He left the car door open as he strode across the lawn, and Diana heard random bits of the chatter between the men. Drywood termites. Fumigation.

Seven days.

Diana's forehead *thunked* against the steering wheel. She hated the curse for what it was doing to her, but what it had brought upon this poor man was worse. She wanted to leave. She wanted to run. But she couldn't do any such thing. Diana and her sisters had wrought a hex upon Miles, and she would do what she had to to ease his pain.

Even if he thought she was a madwoman and a kidnapper.

12

———

Miles stood alone in his tracked-up yard, watching as the men from the pest-control company loaded up and drove away. Diana waited for a moment, letting him gather his composure before she attempted approach. He was a professional. He'd not yelled or screamed, or thrown a tantrum on the ground, but surely by now, that was all Miles Wieland wanted to do.

She stepped out of her car, shutting the driver's door quietly behind her, and walked through the fresh-cut grass toward Miles. It was fall now, the season's cuttings coming fewer and far between, but it wasn't chilly yet. It was cool and crisp and just the sort of weather Diana loved.

Her loafers came to rest beside his work boots, both saddle-leather brown. A bright-red rose petal lay on the earth between them.

Diana looked up at Miles.

He frowned. "They said they tried to call me."

"But your phone was dead," she added helpfully.

"The property management company pushed ahead

without waiting. Something about the rights in the contract fine print, saving their estate before it was overrun." He sighed. "Can't even go in and get my clothes. Everything's locked up in storage, and I don't have access because I wasn't on the rental agreement for the container."

She pursed her lips, staring with him at the blue metal box beside his would-be home. "I could get you some bolt cutters for the lock. Belle's probably got a pair."

He breathed out something that was not really a laugh.

Diana reached for him, letting her fingers twine with his, offering what comfort she could. "I'm sorry, Miles."

He looked into her eyes, held her hand.

"At least—can I give you a ride somewhere?"

He nodded. "I guess I'll need a hotel."

Diana smiled up at him reassuringly, but she was about a thousand percent positive Miles would not find a room. Not with the curse working against him.

She would let him try anyway.

BY THE TIME Miles gave up, it was well past dark. Neither of them said what both were thinking. Miles's phone was still dead for lack of a proper charger, but he'd used Diana's to make half a dozen calls. No one was available. No one had space. Not even a couch. Not even a floor.

"I do have friends," he said to Diana as they sat in the parking lot of their last-resort hotel.

He said it as if he was starting to wonder if it were really true.

She laughed. "It's fine, Miles. I've got room in the apartment, or you can stay at the farmhouse with Bernie." Even as she said it, she knew the latter would be harder to pull off.

Bernie's lifestyle did not lend well to the keeping of secrets. She was nothing but oblivious in the comforts of their childhood home, where witchcraft and magic had been second nature.

"I really wouldn't want to impose any more than I already have."

He'd made several comments about dragging her all over the county to find a place to stay, but Diana hadn't minded at all. Aside from the guilt of Bernie having hexed him and all the horrible things that had happened to Miles because of it, his company had been enjoyable. And as long as they were together—within an arm's length of each other—the curse seemed satisfied. For the time being, anyway. She suspected it would be on some sort of clock, dragging them through more disaster the longer it took to play out. But for now, being close only sent a pleasant hum of magic through her.

"Really," Diana told him, "it's no trouble. Besides, you already spent last night."

He flushed. Diana smiled. She couldn't help it.

"Okay," she said. "Clearly you are not going to accept this on your own, so I'm taking the helm. We are going home, and I'm cooking dinner, and that's the end of it. Tomorrow, you can spend all the time you want figuring out what to do."

Miles didn't argue. He'd already explained that his car was in the repair shop. It had quit on him the day the curse hit, and that was how he'd been downtown near their shop. They'd had no courtesy cars and the rental lot had sold out. He'd been walking... *somewhere* when the storm had chased him into Bad Medicine.

Miles had yet to realize how all these incidents were connected, why they were taking place all at once, so Diana hadn't dwelt on the issue. She did not think Miles was the sort of man who'd easily take her word for it, in any case. He was certainly too rational to believe in magical hexes, even while he was in the grip of one.

"At least let me make dinner," he said.

She smiled genuinely then. "I highly doubt you are more skilled in the kitchen than me, Mr. Wieland." He raised a doubtful brow, and she knew she was right. He'd no apparent intention of challenging her. "I'll let you help." She put the car into reverse and added, "And you can do *all* the dishes."

Miles laughed, and it sounded real. For the first time, it seemed as if he'd given up and finally decided to let his bad day win. The poor, doomed man.

WHEN THEY EVENTUALLY MADE THE drive back to the apartment, the security lamps behind the shop were fully bright. Bernie opened the door for them, on the pretense that she'd just been finishing up. Diana knew the truth, though: Bernie had needed to see for herself that things were okay and that Diana didn't need her to stay.

She'd called six times during the afternoon just to check —the first in a panic when she realized Diana had gone without warning.

Diana gave Bernie a long hug and promised she'd be completely fine. Bernie gave Miles the eye, just in case, then swore to Diana that she'd work all night on the project they had going on. She didn't mention what that project was, exactly. She didn't say she'd be trying to figure out her own hex.

"The shop's locked up tight," she assured Diana. "We've

got two boxes of candles going out by courier tomorrow, and I'll take care of absolutely everything else. Plus, Belle should be back by then."

"Thanks, Bernie. See you in the morning."

Bernie leaned in to whisper, "Call me if anything new happens."

Diana shooed her on her way, ignoring the look Miles gave the odd exchange, and locked the door behind her. She gestured toward the stairs, and Miles obliged.

It was late, and it had been a very long day, so the two of them were quiet as they kicked off their shoes by the wood-carved coat rack at the door and settled in to make dinner. Pasta, Diana had decided, because it was fast and always good.

Miles did seem to know his way around the kitchen well enough, even if he wasn't a pro, and Diana set him the task of chopping vegetables for salad. When she handed him the knife, he hesitated.

"What's wrong?"

He laughed. "Not sure I trust myself after the string of luck I've been having."

She smiled at him. "As long as you're with me, you'll be fine."

The words slipped out before she could stop them, and she turned back to the stove. She was not certain what he thought of her already, but she was pretty sure she did not need to make it any worse with quips like that. If he suspected she was as mad as a hatter, he would be a lot harder to keep contained.

She winced at the idea that she was trying to hold him captive, angling instead for small talk. "So," she said, stopping when she realized it would be bad form to ask him anything about how long he'd lived in town or how he liked Eaton Estates after what had happened to his house. And about his friends or family after she'd heard him call nearly everyone he knew. Or to discuss the weather, given the storms.

She didn't know what was left that was safe, aside from his job. So she said, "How did you end up becoming a fire marshal?"

He drew a stalk of celery out of the colander and sliced it uniformly on the cutting board near the sink beside her. "The usual, I guess. Started as a firefighter, couldn't get along with our lieutenant, couldn't surpass him for the job since he was the captain's nephew. Went sideways instead of up."

Diana grinned as she took a slice of cucumber from his stack. "The usual, huh?"

"It's all I've ever wanted to do," he said. "If I can just avoid conflict in this new situation, I should be fine." There appeared to be more to the story, but he shook it off, changing his tone. "And what about you? How'd you get into the books and herbs business?"

"Our mom, since we were little. And her mother before her. They didn't have a shop, of course, but they'd always grown and healed and traded where they could." The sauce bubbled as she stirred it with the old wooden spoon. It was a hand-me-down, just like everything else that was her favorite in the kitchen. "It was sort of a leap," she admitted, "but we had more than faith. I know I can trust Bernie and Belle, and our family already had a name for itself by then."

He didn't glance up when he said, "Yeah, the old Coulton place. Is that where you said your sister Bernie lives?"

She'd said the farmhouse, not the old Coulton place, but she wasn't surprised that was how he'd heard it. Whether he'd been party to the whispers himself or whether he'd found out when he'd called to check up on her that morning, everyone had a story about the women in that house.

"Yes," Diana said. "Bernie lives there. And no, it's not haunted."

He choked out a breath. "I did not say it was haunted."

"You didn't have to. And besides, ghosts aren't real." Spirits, on the other hand...

He looked up at her then, serious. "I've never heard anything bad about your family, Diana. I'm sorry if it came across that way."

She felt her cheeks color. She'd not meant to let him see it was a sensitive subject. "What, then?" She'd heard bad enough herself, growing up in the town where her family had always been—before it was even a real town. When her mother had tried to send the girls to school with the normal children.

"Only that strange things happened past your trees." He chuckled as he glanced back to his task. "But who am I to judge? My house is wearing a carnival tent."

She bit her lip. "More of a three-ring circus, I think. It's really tragic they decided to go with stripes." She added a pinch more basil to the saucepan. "It could have been something a bit prettier, after all."

He closed his eyes and tilted his head heavenward. "I will never live this down if the guys see it, will I?"

"Ha!" she said. "Not if your friends are anything like my sisters."

His smile said he was glad she'd moved past the darkness he'd brought up.

She had the feeling he regretted he'd been the cause of it. It made her like him just a little bit more.

"Okay," she announced, "bread is coming up in three, two..." She peered through the glass centering the oven door and yanked it open as if presenting whatever awaited behind curtain number three. And it was perfect. Diana could toast bread the exact right amount. Every. Single. Time.

Prue rolled her eyes at them from her spot on the floor, then turned her back to groom a paw. Diana didn't care. She would take her small victories wherever she could get them.

They ate at the small kitchen table that had once been a workstation for Aunt Cilla. Bernie had had to do quite a bit of preparation to make sure it was clean and safe, and they'd sanded down the top few layers just to be certain. Now it sat in the center of her small apartment, looking a size too small for dinner with guests. Miles didn't seem to mind.

He set their plates of salad at each chair, silver utensils beside them. Diana portioned out two bowls of pasta and a heaping basket of bread. "What's your pleasure, Miles? Beer? Wine?"

"Whatever you're having would be fine."

She was pretty sure he meant it. It seemed as though Miles was just grateful to have this day done. She poured a hefty portion of wine for them both, then lifted her glass.

"To new days," she offered.

He clinked the rim of his glass to hers. "To new days." He took a long pull and set the goblet on the table. "Besides," he said, "how could tomorrow possibly be any worse?"

Diana forced a smile, brushing a wayward rose petal off the edge of the table. "Well," she said, "at least there's that."

13

Diana had watched Miles as he ate, the way he absently turned his fork, the way his careful fingers tore each bite of bread. She'd been thinking about the curse since its portents began. She'd been wondering how to stop it. How to let it run its course.

Maybe Bernie had just willed them to get ... *together.* Maybe that was all it would take. Her sister had been pretty drunk, after all. Maybe she'd just wanted to give her a quick tumble in the sheets. It was possible Diana could do this one thing and the hex would let Miles go.

Some small part of her wanted her to avoid it, to keep him there with her as long as she could. She shoved the thought down, hating the ugliness of it. She was no seductress. No dark fairy-tale witch.

She did not need a curse to get a man.

But no matter how much she hated the part of her that wanted to cave to those fears, the other part was worse. The part that wanted to actually do it. The part that told her even now to reach out to him, that wanted to feel his hands on her, to take him to her bed. It terrified her. It called to her. She did not want to take advantage of some poor man who had been drawn there by a hex. She was not the kind of witch who meant to ravish a stranger.

But Miles did not feel like a stranger. Diana didn't know if it was that they were getting on so well or the curse. She might never know. And what if it didn't work, if she fell into those desires and Bernie's intent was not satisfied—Miles would not be free. He would only be tied to Diana further.

She glanced up at him as she dried the last plate, the dish towel in her hand embroidered with a single tiny leaf. Miles's expression was relaxed, his attention on the glass and the soap and the business at hand. Surely this was not the demeanor of a man destroyed by a curse. He was still making his own decisions, wasn't he? Even if the weather and the termites had narrowed his options down considerably. He rinsed the goblet and passed it to her, catching her eye as he did. Their skin touched, his warm from the washing but not unnaturally so. The tingle was there still, but Diana was fairly certain the curse had nothing to do with the warmth in her belly.

She'd let her hand rest against his too long, and Miles noticed. The look he gave her was something of a question, something of a response. She knew what her own expression was saying. Gods, she couldn't help it. No matter the curse, no matter the consequences, she wanted to be closer to Miles. She wanted to know what it felt like to kiss him. He would be good at it, she was sure. And it had been so long since she'd had a good, serious, satisfying sort of kiss.

The warmth in her belly spread, and Miles's finger slid forward on her arm as he shifted closer. She knew her neck had flushed. She knew he knew what she was thinking. She could practically taste him, practically feel his mouth on hers. They were so close it was painful, and she only wanted to be nearer.

Miles took a breath, suddenly seeming to realize what was about to happen. His brow drew down again, back to that consternation from the previous day. It said, *What am I doing?*

Diana glanced down under the pretense of drying the glass in her hand. She understood why he'd drawn away. He'd said it enough times. He thought he was taking advantage of her. Some strange man just showing up at her place. Forcing himself onto her couch for a stay—and now forcing himself onto her.

He was so wrong.

The curse wasn't going to do everything for her. It had gotten a man there. In the shop. In her apartment. In the normally heavily guarded six-inch window of her own personal space. There was only so much it could do.

If Diana wanted Miles Wieland, she was going to have to finish it herself.

Miles passed her the last glass then drained the soapy water in the sink. Chore completed, he turned to her, and for a moment they stood face-to-face. He pressed a hand to his chest, leaned forward as if to bow.

"Thank you, again, for your overly generous hospitality. I am sure you're ready to have me out of your hair." His gaze caught on her hair, long and loose, and Miles swallowed before going on. "I won't be a bother to you any longer, Diana."

"It's no bother," she said softly. She laid the dish towel over the rack. "Let me get you a toothbrush at least. I keep some spare supplies around on the off-chance Belle or

Bernie might spend the night. New ones," she added lamely.

He smiled. "New would be great."

Diana went to the cupboard and took out one of the packages, laid it on the vanity with toothpaste and a clean hand towel. When she came back out, Miles was standing in the center of her living area, entirely too big for the narrow space. She brushed her palms against her jean legs, ignoring Prue looping between her calves. "Well, I guess you can see I don't have a television, so that's out. But you're welcome to listen to music if it will help you sleep." She showed him the radio and clicked on the couch-side lamp, then moved the throw pillows to the adjacent chair. There was an ottoman beside it, where it had been moved out of the way for the sisters' earlier spellcasting, and Diana opened it to take out a woven throw and an heirloom quilt. "Not sure if you like it warm or…" She held up both, and Miles took them from her hands.

"Thank you, Diana. Really. But you've done enough."

She stared at him nervously.

"I'll be entirely fine."

Diana hoped it was true.

She clicked off the main lights and trod barefoot to her room. She did not glance back to look at him. She bit her lip as she locked the bedroom door.

It was two a.m. when she woke, roused by a shuffling sound coming from the other room. She walked through familiar darkness toward her door, bare-legged beneath an old Stones T-shirt, hair drawn back in a loose ponytail. She peered into the living room.

Miles was on the couch, blankets tangled around him as he thrashed against some unseen force. Heart in her throat, she ran to him, certain he'd been caught in magic's snare. But as she reached the couch, she did not feel the tingle of magic, no sign of the hex at work. He went still. She hovered over him, unsure what to do. He called out, his arm swinging wide. It smacked into her bare leg, and he shot up, clutching her leg and panting, and Diana realized it had only been a nightmare.

She remembered the dreams. The man trapped within a fire. It had been him.

He had needed her.

Miles stared at her, suddenly alert, chest heaving, palm on her skin.

Her heart thundered along with his as she stared back, void of all sensation aside from his touch.

"It was you." The rasped words seemed to have been torn from him, quiet and rough.

"It's still me," she whispered. Something passed between them, wild and untamable, and Miles's grip tightened. Heat shot through Diana. All the nervousness she'd felt earlier was gone, there was nothing she wanted more than to touch him. Her bare leg shifted as she climbed onto his lap, nothing between them but the tangle of a woven throw. Miles was shirtless, his chest clean of the ink that marked his shoulder. His palms slid up her thighs where she straddled him, clasping to draw her closer and sending electricity through every nerve ending in her body.

The only light in the room was from the far window, where moonlight and a nearby streetlamp let in a soft glow. The light caught in Miles's gaze. It seemed to burn right into Diana's soul.

She reached up to touch him, to drag a thumb across his bottom lip, down the line of his jaw. The way she'd done in his dream, when his face had been obscured by shadow. There was something raw between them, so separate from everything she'd worried about the day before. She was filled with the cool surety she only felt when working a time-worn spell. She knew what she was doing, what she wanted.

And Diana didn't think she'd ever wanted anything as much as she wanted Miles in that moment.

She leaned forward, fingers sliding into his hair as his mouth opened beneath hers. Her hands stole down his chest as she reveled in the heat of him, the feel of his touch.

She rocked closer, skin touching skin. The tingle of magic was only background noise to the blood roaring in her ears. Diana's desire washed over her, burning her flesh until it screamed to be free. She drew her shirt over her head, then tossed it to the floor.

Miles took in the sight of her, his desire bare.

Nothing could have made her want him more. She leaned into him, pressing hard against his length, teasing his bottom lip with her tongue. His able hands caressed her back, her thighs, then slipped the band from her hair to let it fall free. He stared up at her, sliding the band onto his wrist as his palms traced a line down her sides, over her hips. "Miles," she breathed, and he grabbed her by the waist to roll her onto her back on the cushions.

She lay bare before him, lifting her arms over her head as he leaned down to kiss her neck. His mouth skimmed over her, teasing and tortuous before his gaze slid back to hers, asking if she was sure. If this was what she wanted.

"Yes," she vowed. It was the surest she'd ever been. She

leaned forward to give him a deep, lingering kiss, then lay back onto the cushions to slide her legs around his waist.

She had every intention of being as close to Miles as she could get.

Even if it was only temporary.

Even if it was only tonight.

14

————————

Diana woke when the midmorning sun made its way through her living room blinds, casting thin rays of light right into her eyes. She scrunched them tighter for a moment and then realized the utter comfort and warmth she was feeling was coming from another person. Her breath seized, even while her body felt like jelly. Miles lay behind her, an arm around her waist where he'd pulled her tight against him, every possible inch of skin touching skin. His other arm was beneath her like a pillow, his hand dangling off the edge of askew cushions.

Her hairband was still around his wrist.

Diana let out a breath. She was not ashamed of what she'd done to Miles, exactly, but she knew it wasn't really right. Never mind that they had been perfect together. He'd been led there by the curse. None of it was real.

It didn't count.

Wilted red rose petals lay scattered across the floorboards, reminding her that the curse had not been satisfied.

Whatever Bernie had willed of it, a romp on the sofa had not been the resolution—no matter how incredible it had been.

They'd lain awake in the hours before dawn, gentle murmurs of apology from Miles as he'd tried to explain the nightmares that had plagued him and how he hadn't meant to take advantage of the situation. And soft kisses from Diana as she'd attempted to ease the echoes of a long-ago pain, of fires that still burned in his memories, and as she had tried not to be eaten by guilt that the curse was the only reason they'd been in the situation at all.

Bernie's hex had brought her a man who'd needed healing, but Diana had never been good at matters of the heart.

She missed her mother so badly. Diana wanted to breathe in the scent of her, to read a new faded letter, one that had come just for her and would help to ease her heart through troubled times. The way they always did.

She slid out from Miles's grip, swiping the petals out of their pattern with a bare foot in case he were to wake before she was back with a broom. He would surely be up soon, given his normal job requirements, except that the last few days had been so rough on him.

She drew her shirt over her head, glancing into her bedroom to see Prue settled like royalty in the center of the otherwise empty bed.

Diana rolled her eyes and muttered, "Glad to see I was missed."

She crept toward the kitchen, nearly jumping out of her skin when she caught sight of Belle, arms crossed, perched on a stool by the counter.

"So we're just giving up on looking for a cure?"

Diana shushed her sister vigorously, glancing over a

shoulder at Miles on the couch. He'd shifted to his stomach, face buried into a throw pillow. The tattoo on his shoulder howled at the ceiling.

Diana looked back at Belle helplessly. "Of course we aren't giving up. I just—I—What are you doing here?"

"Checking on you," Belle said. "Apparently, I'm a little late."

Diana rubbed a palm over her face.

"Didn't work, I take it?"

"No," Diana answered beneath her palm. She would not admit that she'd not done it for the sake of the curse. The fact remained that a cure was nowhere in sight. She sighed, hand dropping. "I don't know what to do. Belle, you should see what it did yesterday..." She glanced over her shoulder again. Miles was homeless, vehicleless, and practically friendless since the curse had let loose on him.

"I know," Belle said. "I talked to Bernie about a dozen times during the afternoon." She frowned at Diana's expression and the obvious distress rolling off her. "Listen, Bernie's been doing some research, and we have a few leads. I'm going to head up to Riverton. No promises, Di, but I'll do what I can."

Belle stood, throwing her small leather backpack over one shoulder, and Diana let her feel the gratefulness inside of her. Belle nodded and lowered a brow. "Keep hold of yourself, sister."

Diana would. She knew she had to. It was all too easy to get washed away in the current of a hex—to forget who you were and what mattered.

She cleared up the rose petals from their pattern on the floor, jumped in the shower for a quick rinse, and tied her hair back into a braided bun. When she came out of the bathroom in jeans and a black silk blouse fifteen minutes later, Miles was sleeping on his back, one hand splayed on his bare chest, the other arm crossed over his head. Part of her wanted to go to him, to crawl right back into his embrace.

But that wasn't Diana. She would remember herself, no matter how tempting it was to do otherwise. If Diana was anything, she was responsible. Dependable. She crept through the door, leaving it open just a crack for Prue.

The shop was dark, the sounds of the street outside muffled by distance and glass. Diana put the coffee on to brew, drew two pencils out of the cup on the counter, poked one into her bun, and bit down on the other as she clicked the shop lights on and made her way to the front door.

It was nine o'clock on a Thursday, and Bad Medicine was open for business. She turned the hand-painted sign to *Open*, smiling like a fool, the same way she always did at the task. She checked stock of the lavender and lemongrass and a few of the other best-selling supplies, adjusted the cut-flower display, and realigned the carved totems on their shelf. Bernie had done a good job keeping things straight the day before, despite having spent half her time searching through old family texts. Diana hoped that whatever she'd found, whatever Belle was going to Riverton to hunt down, would pay off for her and Miles. The longer she waited, the more tricks the curse played, the bigger the risk of getting caught.

Of losing everything.

Diana's stomach dipped at the thought—at the idea not just of losing the shop but of being run out of town. Of having to leave their family home and go into hiding.

Of what the hex might do to Miles.

She shook herself, pouring a cup of coffee into her favorite Thursday mug and sliding her notebook closer as she settled on the register counter stool to start her to-do list. She was halfway through her cup and halfway down the list when the front door chimed open. Diana glanced up with an automatic customer-friendly smile, then froze.

Abigail.

Brown.

Abby hates-the-Coultons-on-a-mission-to-destroy-everything Brown stood in the open doorway of Bad Medicine Books & Herbs, her hair drawn back too tightly and her skirt-suit silhouette too perfect.

Diana's pencil cracked beneath her thumb. She held still for a moment, as if it might only be a mistake and Abby had taken a wrong turn.

"Diana," Abby said, destroying that tenuous strand of hope.

Diana cursed, but only mentally. She stood slowly, easing toward the end of the counter as she decided the best way to usher the woman out. "Abby. So good to see you. What can I do for you today?"

Abby smirked and threw a disdainful gaze at the racks lining the store. She was coming closer, approaching the register and Diana. Diana had a moment of panic, doing a mental assessment of her surroundings and any incriminating evidence that might be visible. But Bernie had assured her everything was in order.

Abby strode to the opposite side of the counter, stopping exactly eighteen inches short of where a normal customer might stand, as if she was loath to touch anything. "I'm not here to shop," she said. Unnecessarily.

Diana tilted her head to gesture, *Go on.*

"I'm looking for someone. One of our county officials has gone missing, and we have reason to believe he was last here."

Diana felt the color drain from her face.

Abby's expression grew sharp at the change. Diana didn't have the talent her sister did, but she could tell Abby had not been concerned for the missing man. She was only pleased to find a Coulton guilty in the process.

"I thought so," Abby purred. "So, Miss Coulton, shall I bring in the police or—"

"Police?" Diana choked out. "What—why would you need the police?" Not because Diana and her sister had knocked out a man, discussed shoving him in the trunk of her painfully uncool sedan, knocked him out again, inadvertently broken his car, filled his house with wood-boring insects...

Abby shook her head as if she was dealing with an imbecile. "Miles Wieland has been missing from his post for two days. Your family has always been suspect, Diana, but to think you'd go as far as to—"

There was a thump on the stairs behind her—Prue coming down and through the corridor too fast, Diana thought. She did not turn around to verify that fact until she saw the shock on Abby's face.

Not Prue.

Miles.

Diana stared at him. Aside from the sleeves rolled up his thick forearms and a woman's hairband crossing his wrist, he was dressed and proper, looking for all the world as if he'd shown up to report to work, not simply come down because he'd woken up alone or smelled fresh coffee brewing below. He took one look at her expression, and Diana could tell he remembered her fears about inspection and the shop. He could have no idea that fear had escalated to include arrest.

"Abby," he said coolly. "What brings you here?"

Abby was momentarily at a loss for words apparently, but Diana managed a cold, "She's looking for you."

Miles's gaze returned to Abby. Abby shrugged and gestured vaguely. "Council asked me to drop by this morning," she offered. "Just to check on you on my way through. Terrible what's happened at your place, Miles. Everyone is so concerned."

Diana gaped at her. The woman had just implied Miles was missing, but clearly she'd already heard about his home —and probably the fact that Miles had called nearly everyone he knew asking for a place to stay only the afternoon before.

Miles stepped closer, crossed his arms. "I'm fine, Abby. I'd say you could tell the council the same, but I've already reported in myself."

She flushed and then recovered. "Chip said you were hurt. That you'd hit your head. You look okay."

Miles's gaze turned hard.

Abby threw a pointed glance at Diana. "Evidently you've got something else keeping you from your work."

Miles leaned forward just the slightest bit, and a thrill shot through Diana. She tamped it down. It should not thrill her. None of this should. Miles said, "Last time I checked, Abigail, it was not your business how I spend my personal days."

Diana thought she might literally die. Right there on the shop floor. Without even having finished her coffee.

Abby straightened. "I assure you, as head of the town council, it is entirely my business. And if Chip hadn't insisted that I look into the matter—" She pressed her lips together then went on. "Mister Wieland, if we could only continue this discussion outside, I—"

"There's nothing to discuss," Miles said.

Abby blew a breath out her nose like an overly thin, heavily powdered dragon. "Not regarding your"—her gaze roamed over Diana—"*personal* time, no. But urgent council business, I assure you."

Miles stared at Abby for a long moment, then brushed past her toward the front door. Abby turned to hurry after him, the confident stride she'd mastered showing a minor fault.

Diana watched from her spot as the woman rushed out behind Miles, heels clicking, and slammed the door behind them both. Diana moaned, loudly and horribly, and slammed her head onto the deskpad on the counter. A minute later, there was a muffled *thwump* as Prue landed on the countertop. She gave Diana a purring nuzzle before getting distracted with a tendril of Diana's hair.

Diana rolled her face to the side, cheek pressed against her schedule, and looked up pitifully at the cat. "Is there not something one of us can do about that horrible woman?"

Prue sneezed, shook her head, and planted both paws in front of her to stare at Diana.

"I know," Diana said. "Priorities. Your breakfast first, my life crisis later."

She turned to go toward the workshop so she could fill the cat's bowl and was nearly knocked off her feet at a sudden flash of light and concussion from the front of the store. She jerked around to look; the bottles lining the wall had been rattled, but nothing had shattered. She realized it had not been inside the building at all. It had been outside.

It had been the hex. *Miles.*

15

———————

Miles had woken that morning on a strange couch in the middle of a sunlit room, certain his night had been a dream. It was too perfect not to have been, besides that he'd dreamed of the selfsame woman for days. No matter how real it had seemed, he could not quite convince himself she'd walked into his life. Or, he into hers, he supposed. Because Miles could not bring himself to give her distance, not since the night of the storm.

He had run hand over his face, groaning as he recalled his house and that he did not have a car. Then he'd seen the thin black band on his wrist and thought that maybe it had all been worth it. He scanned the room, but he knew she'd gone downstairs. He could smell coffee brewing, and realized with a wince that it was well past time for him to have been at work. But he'd already explained his situation to the office the night before. He might have wanted to go in, but he still had to figure out where to stay and how to get his possessions from the container.

Miles had stood to cross to the bathroom and had the

strangest sensation of a remembered conversation. The raven-haired sister, he thought, but he had no idea why. *So we're just giving up on looking for a cure?* Miles slid a palm over his bare chest, glancing toward the kitchen. Had he dreamed that too? Or was Diana—his stomach dropped—was Diana sick?

He had splashed his face in the bathroom sink, trying to clear his head. He didn't know what was happening. It was like he couldn't trust himself. Nothing made sense. He had stared at himself in the mirror, only one thing true and clear. He needed to see Diana.

She was only downstairs.

But when Miles had started down the stairs, he'd heard the echo of conversation. He wasn't certain she would want him traipsing through her shop, fresh out of her apartment where they'd done incredibly pleasant things, but as he paused, he had recognized the voice. Abbigail Brown. And worse, she was in the middle of accusing Diana of a crime, using the very Coulton family gossip that had clearly hurt Diana the night before.

He had stepped hard into the corridor, drawing Abby's attention away from her prey. When Diana had turned, he remembered something else, the offhand comments about the trouble she'd had with her shop, the quick report Chip had given over the phone about what seemed numerous frivolous violations.

By the time Abby had tried to drag him outside on false pretenses, he was ready enough to go. Not because he cared about her supposed concern, but because he had every intention of straightening the woman out. She'd rushed to catch up to him, her heels clicking on the concrete sidewalk as Miles put distance between the storefront and their confrontation. He gritted his teeth when Abby's manicured nails latched onto his sleeve.

Miles spun, expression hard. Abby snatched her hand back but did not move away. "Miles," she hissed. "You don't know what you're getting into. Those women—those—those,"

Miles had the sense Abby was working up to a word she was going to regret. He cut her off. "Stop. My personal life is none of your business. You have so far overstepped boundaries that—"

Abby grabbed at him again. "No!" Her tone was vehement, but she could not seem to get a grasp on what she wanted to say.

"Spit it about, Abby. Neither of us has time for this."

She shook her head. "Miles, those women, they aren't… safe." She glanced over her shoulder then tugged his arm.

Miles stood fast, jerking free of her grip. He had a strange foreboding about the entire ordeal, and he really didn't know how his life had gone so sideways in a matter of days. He was standing on the street arguing with a coworker about a woman he'd met in his dreams. Somehow, the confrontation with Abby seemed the more bizarre of the two situations, a fact he would have to worry about later. "You need to get yourself under control," he told her. "I don't know what you think you're accomplishing here, but—"

Abby whipped out her cellphone and started to dial. "I'm going to show you," she hissed. "I'll show you and then you'll see. You're coming with me, Miles. I'm putting an end to this now."

Miles glanced toward the shop, terrified at the idea Diana might witness any part of their scene. Abby's hand was on him again, but when he glanced back to set her straight, a blast so bright it might have been lightning—had it not been violet—lit up the midday street. An explosion of what felt like electricity shot through him, cracking against the buildings and shattering the bulb at the top of the light pole.

Miles blinked, stunned, certain he had not just seen what he thought he saw. But before him, where Abigail Brown had been standing, there was nothing but *gone*.

Diana ran toward the front of the store, sick at the idea of what might be waiting for her. She'd thought Abby had only meant to take Miles outside, that she'd keep him within a safe distance for the curse. They must have gone farther. She must have dragged him far enough away or done something else—something to interfere and threaten the outcome of the curse.

Diana couldn't think of it, couldn't bear to see what she might find, but there was no stopping her feet as they moved of their own accord. She had to find him.

Had to save Miles.

She burst out the front door of the shop. The buzz of magic streaked across her exposed skin and zipped down her spine. She held her breath, afraid to get spirited away with the power of it, her head jerking to find Miles.

He stood at the end of the long sidewalk, arms limp at his sides, eyes wide. He didn't appear to be hurt, but something was very wrong.

Diana moved toward him, forcing herself not to run. She had to pay attention, be alert for whatever the hex had wrought.

She had to get close enough to Miles to satisfy it.

He stared at her, and as Diana came near, she studied him for signs of distress, searching his brown eyes, his sharp jaw, the clean cut of his dark hair. He seemed intact, physically anyway. She kept moving, his eyes only clearing when she reached him, stood right before him, and took hold of his hand.

"Miles, what happened?"

He shook his head.

"Miles," she repeated, steady pressure on his palms, the tingle of magic between them like static on the air. The expression on his face hurt Diana, caused her physical pain. She winced while attempting to ignore the ache in her chest and think purposeful, positive thoughts.

To refocus.

"I'm here, Miles. I'm here."

His gaze settled on hers for a long moment, then he looked around them, taking in the storefronts lining the street, the trees placed at regular intervals, the wrought-iron railing that decorated each block. "Abby," he said. "It took Abby."

Diana whipped around to search their surroundings, having momentarily forgotten Abby was even involved. "Who?" she snapped.

He didn't answer, and she yanked his hand. "Who, Miles? Who took Abby?"

His mouth came open, but he did not speak.

Diana could see it in his soul. *It*, he'd said. Not they. *It* took Abby.

The magic.
Miles knew.
Miles had seen it.
And Abby was gone.

17

Abby really was gone.

Diana had searched up and down the street, examined the sidewalk for traces of whatever the magic had wrought, and forced Miles to dial the woman's cell number from Diana's phone on the off chance they would hear it ring. Nothing had worked. Abigail Brown was missing and what had taken her had left no sign.

Miles had only said she had disappeared. There had been a flash of light—like lightning, he'd said—and then... nothing. Nothing at all.

Bernie was on her way. She'd texted Diana shortly after the flash of light, not because she'd seen it from outside of town but because she'd felt Diana's distress. Belle had called, but the message was short.

Go dark, she'd said. *Stay safe.*

Diana paced in front of the worktable, wringing her hands as wilted rose petals crunched beneath her feet. She'd dragged Miles back into the shop, convinced whatever she needed to track Abby was inside. She was positive standing on the corner like the guilty party was not the most brilliant tactic. Diana could not go dark. Not yet. She could not bear to leave everything behind.

She would fix it.

She would do whatever she had to do.

"We have to call the police," Miles said again.

He'd been watching her pace and repeating his demand they notify someone the woman was gone. He didn't understand any of it. And Diana could tell his concern was shifting back to wariness, that he was remembering his own near disappearance only days before and that none of the women had called the authorities on him or the paramedics for him.

"Just one more minute," she told Miles. "I have to think."

He stood, taking hold of her by the shoulders and forcing her to still. To look him in the eye. "I know you're in shock, but—"

She threw up her hands. "I'm not in shock. I'm just trying to figure out what to do."

"We call the law. Now, Diana. It has to be now."

She growled. "Stop saying that. Just stop."

He reached across her in an attempt to steal back her phone. She jerked it away. "What do you think will happen?" she snapped. "What do you think the police will say when you tell them she just disappeared in a flash of purple lightning?"

"It doesn't matter. I will tell them. Every second counts in cases like this—"

"Cases like this?" she shouted. "Miles, there *are* no cases like this."

"She didn't just disappear," he told her. "Something—somehow—" He threw up his own hands. "Look, I don't know what happened. I don't know what's going on with my head or why—" His voice cut off as his gaze caught on hers. He flushed. Diana was sure he was thinking of the curse now. He just didn't understand that was what it was, what was causing him to be drawn to her. To think of her with every breath, every beat of his heart. "I only know that the *only* thing I have to do is call this in. It's all that matters."

Diana shook her head. "No. You don't get it. So much more matters. All of it."

He came at her again to get the phone, and she yanked back, knocking into a display as Prue leapt between them, hissing. The shoulder of Diana's blouse was soaked with something rancid as glass bottles shattered to the ground.

She cursed.

A real one.

Her hand slapped over her mouth, but it was too late. Seven brown toads plopped onto the ground before her feet.

"Oh, for a black duck's sake," Diana moaned.

Miles leapt back, stumbled, pointed toward the ground. "What was that?"

He was yelling, the semblance of calm he'd mustered earlier entirely absent. She rubbed a palm over her face. What had she even said in the first place?

"*Remedium videtur ranae,*" she tried. No, that wasn't it. "*Remedium sponsione ranarum.*"

The third try she nearly got it, and the mass of small toads leapt into one exceptionally squat amphibian as Miles stared on in horror. Prue struck out a paw after the giant toad, and the thing shuffled its hulking mass under a low shelf.

"Stop that!" Diana told the cat. Prue glared up at her, planted her bottom on the floor, and wrapped her tail in a perfect arc around her front legs.

Well, that was brilliant. All that time working to keep their secret, and not only had the curse stolen Abby right before Miles's eyes, but Diana had just done magic in front of him.

And not the mysterious love hex kind. The obvious, terrifying, defies-reality kind.

Miles had stopped yelling, at least, but his mouth hung open as he gaped at her. She was considering how best to explain—or to detour him further—when he dropped to the floor to peer under the cabinet at the toad.

Diana shuffled sideways, out of the man's way, but he paid her no mind.

He was searching for the source. As if it were fire. Life had taught him that disasters could be tracked back to a cause, that the smoke and char could be followed to an origin point, to a catalyst.

Magic was elemental, but nothing like what Miles knew and understood. He was seeking out answers he would never find.

When Miles drew back and shifted to his knees to look up at her, Diana knew it was not the source of a worldly thing that he had found. Not the spark of a fire he came back with.

It was only the ashes of his faith. The loss of his foundations.

"You did this," he whispered.

"Miles," she started, but it was too late. He was scuffling to his feet, scrambling away from her. She rolled her neck and sighed. She did not have the energy for this.

He bumped into the rack of shelves behind him. It was plain he was getting ready to bolt for the door.

"If you hold very still, I will explain it to you." Her words sounded more like a threat than she'd meant them, but Diana was running out of patience for the entire day.

Miles's eyes widened, his hands going stealthily to the shelf behind him. Looking for another weapon, Diana supposed.

Probably good he had no idea how dangerous the herbs and powders surrounding them could actually be. "Miles," she said again, calmly, "I need you to stay here."

It was the wrong thing to say. He shot a hand toward her, finger pointed. "Stay away from me. Whatever you're doing —whatever this is—" His brows lowered, face crumpling. "How did you get inside my head? What did you do to me?"

Whatever Diana had planned to say plummeted to the pit of her stomach.

Miles shook himself again, shifting a foot closer to the front of the store.

The back door slammed open, followed by Bernie calling out as she rushed through the corridor. Miles took the chance, running full tilt for the front entrance.

Diana watched, fully expecting some sort of retaliation, but the magic didn't stop him. Miles had every intention of leaving, and the hex—for some reason Diana didn't under-stand—let him go.

Diana turned to Bernie, open-mouthed. Her sister's expression was flat.

"What's going to happen?" Diana said. "What will it do to him?" All she could think of was what had happened earlier to Abby. The flash of light. Miles saying *she's gone*.

"It's only a spell, Di. The magic can't hold him that hard. If he decides to break it, it will give him some rope."

"And then snap his neck when it jerks him back?" Diana asked.

Bernie frowned. "He won't go that far. He doesn't under-stand, is all."

Diana stared out the front windows of the shop, the shadows of midday small beneath the sun. "It's not that he doesn't understand. It's that he doesn't *believe*." Magic wasn't real to Miles, couldn't fit within his carefully ordered world. He would think it was a trick. Deception. He would only fight it more.

He would never trust Diana again.

Her sister's reply was quiet. "So that's what you'll do, Diana. You'll help him believe."

18

Diana sat with her sisters around a small wooden table, staring at a wide glass bowl. Bernie had filled the basin with water she'd been collecting from a spring in the woods, and Belle had added a summoning or two. The drapes were drawn over the windows, as it was well past sunset, and twenty-seven candles flickered around the room, their glow catching on glass bottles lining the workshop shelves.

Miles had called the authorities to report Abby missing, but his friends had been more concerned that he had no explanation for how she'd disappeared and about the way he'd seemed confused and oddly shaken. Not to mention why he'd been on a street on the outskirts of town meeting with Abby when she'd told everyone else she was going to a stylist appointment on the other side of town.

Belle had done her reconnaissance via cell phone during her drive home, calling on her contacts at the local sheriff's office. She'd been told few details but understood the men might not have entirely trusted Miles's lack of explanation of the chain of events and that they'd followed up with standard procedures, checking with local hospitals, friends, and family. Because Miles could not say that anything had actually happened to her beyond his sketchily detailed flash-of-light rantings, they didn't really have good reason to suspect foul play. But they did know Miles and did have concern for Abby, so they'd been doing more than they might have otherwise, recent head injury of their sole witness notwithstanding.

They had not yet shown up to interview Diana. The sisters didn't know exactly what that meant. But if they could find Abby soon, somehow call her back before she'd missed work the next morning or anyone became more concerned, there was still a chance to save their comfortable lives and their family home.

Belle had no luck with the witches she'd met in Riverton, but the hex had become suddenly less pressing than the trouble they might be in for a missing woman. Belle had argued for skipping town, but guilt had Bernie taking Diana's side. That made it two against one, and Belle had acquiesced, so there they sat, three witches in the back of an herb shop watching what was supposed to be a scrying bowl.

"What now?" Bernie whispered.

"I don't know," Belle hissed. "I told you I've never done this before."

The dark water was still, its surface like a sheet of glass.

"Let's sing," Diana suggested.

Bernie shrugged. "Worth a shot."

They took each other's hands, palms over one and under the other, to create a circle. Belle started, a low hum that Bernie and Diana followed before she broke into words. The candles flickered then flared brighter. Flower petals blew onto the table, scattering across the water in the bowl. They were snowdrop petals from the shelf on the far wall. Diana remembered a legend about them, something about drops of blood, but blood was the last thing she should be thinking of. She focused harder on the singing, on not being distracted yet again. Belle's voice rose, carrying the melody above her sisters' chant.

The water rippled.

The three women leaned forward.

They would find Abby, Diana thought. This would work, and their worries would be over.

The water turned murky, clouding to black like ink dropped into the bowl. Fog rose from the bottom, bubbling up from some place that was deeper than the depth of their vessel. Movement slid beneath the haze, a shifting flicker behind the clouds.

Abby. It was Abby.

Belle squeezed Diana's hand, reminding her to stay with the spell. She released a breath, let her song fall back in with the others, and watched the basin for what it would tell.

Abby was moving through something dark, running her hands over a wall to find her way. They caught a glimpse of block and stone, somewhere industrial, somewhere not well lit. Her hair had fallen from its coif, a thin strand of blonde damp against her cheek. She was searching, looking for something Diana could not see. The water rippled, the image breaking into lines, and Bernie's tone went shaky.

They needed this to work.

They had to find her.

The water changed its hue, and Abby's eyes shifted down as she reached out. She was grabbing a handle, opening a door. Flickering light hit her face.

The sisters jumped as the back door banged open, rattling through the shop.

A woman's shrill voice cut through the silence as she cursed.

Abby.

There, in the shop. Abigail Brown burst into the workshop, heedless of whatever locks and protections the women had set. Because they had called her there.

Bernie's face went white as she looked at Belle. "I think you did it wrong."

Abby glared down at them where they sat, guilty by all appearances of at least some kind of strange water worship. Belle slid the bowl sideways, and Diana swiped a hand over the top to clear the snowdrop petals. Water. It was only water now.

Abby pointed a long, manicured finger at them. "*You.*"

Diana swallowed hard, though she was fairly certain Belle would be receiving most of the woman's blame, just on principle.

Bernie brushed a knuckle across her nose, slid her glasses further back on her head. She turned to face Abby full on. "Abigail! How are you?"

Abby didn't even spare her a look. Her ire was directed at the strange raven-haired beauty who had stolen every man she'd ever loved. "You did this."

"Did what?" Bernie said. "Abby, where have you been? What are you doing here?"

Diana cleared her throat and took up Bernie's direction. "Are you all right? We heard—Abby, do you know there are people looking for you? Worried about you?"

Abby blanched. "What did you do to me?" She shook

with rage, her fists slamming down to her sides. "How long have I even been missing?"

Belle leaned back, crossed her arms. "Give it a rest, Abby. You were only gone a few hours. But seriously, *this* is the place you choose to come when you know people are searching for you?"

Bernie turned to stare at Belle, eyes wide and pleading. Belle ignored her.

"Why are you constantly trying to bring your laws down on us? It was *one* guy."

Abby's face flushed scarlet, her fingers curling into claws. "One guy? One guy, Arabelle?"

Belle's jaw flexed. She hated when anyone who wasn't family used her given name. "Get over yourself, Abby."

The color fell from Abby's skin, and Diana understood why. Belle had said Abby's name properly, but she'd used the tone none of them would ever forget: the tone of an entire class of second-graders taunting *Scabby Abby* for months on end.

Abby said, "You will pay for this, Arabelle Coulton. Mark my words."

Belle stood, the legs of her chair squealing across the hardwood floor. "Is that a threat?"

Diana was on her feet, hand pressing Belle's forearm, as Bernie backed closer to Abby.

Abby's voice was low, an oath. "I remember what you did."

"Look," Diana said, "I know you've been through a lot— or something—Abby. But you should call Miles. Go to the police station, let everyone know you're okay."

At the mention of Miles, some of the heat returned to

Abby's cold expression. "What do you care about Miles, Diana? Like he'd ever be interested in you."

Diana felt her own color rise, but not in anger. It was the shame of knowing it might be true, that Miles would have never been with her if not for the hex.

Belle scoffed. "Like you know what a man wants."

Abby shoved into Bernie on her way to Belle. Bernie's glasses fell to the ground, and Prue screeched into the room, barreling past the women to jump onto the table. The basin slid off the edge, splattering spelled water across the floor and counter. Prue jumped the other direction, and Diana realized—too late—that the cat was chasing dark wisps of smoke through the air.

"What is that?" Abby whispered. She was backing up, her fingers grasping Bernie's arm.

Bernie gaped at the thing Prue chased then at Diana. Bernie and the cat had about the same level of composure in an emergency. It was neither's strong suit.

Diana shook her head. "Bernie, you know what, I think we should take Abby to the hospital. Clearly she's not well—"

Abby's gaze shot to Diana, and she seemed to realize she was holding Bernie's arm. She recoiled, wiping her palms on her skirt. Bernie blinked at her, apparently too insulted to speak.

"No," Abby said, pointing toward the sisters. "You stay away from me. All of you." She was backing up again, as if afraid to turn on the sisters or the cat or whatever she was seeing that looked like, perhaps, sentient black smoke. She pointed again. "I mean it. Away."

She made it to the corridor before she turned to run. Diana smacked her palms over her face and slumped into her chair. Prue screeched again, leaping from counter to shelf, and causing a half-dozen containers to rattle to the workspace below.

"You can't catch it, doll," Bernie told the cat. She reached for Prue, cradling her around the middle to draw her to her chest. She rubbed behind the cat's ears. "It's an omen, is all. You have to let it go."

Diana felt the last bit of strength seep out of her.

Belle put a hand on her sister's shoulder. "Don't worry, Di. We'll figure it out."

She was wrong. Diana could feel it. They'd wrecked things good and truly. Things were well past just figuring out. The hex had wrought bad magic. Miles had seen it. Abby had seen it. The authorities would be seeking them out. And, after everything else, an omen.

"What's it telling you?" Diana asked Belle. "The omen— what is it warning of?"

Belle turned away before answering. Her tone was clipped. "Dead roses."

Diana thought of the wilting petals, their edges going black. Petals that had started showing up soft and bright, that now crunched beneath her feet.

They were on a countdown, and they were running out of time.

19

———

Miles stood stock-still as Tommy shone a lighted scope into each of his eyes. It was the first time Miles had stopped pacing since he'd left Diana's side. His hands still trembled and he shoved them into his pockets.

"I don't know, man," Tommy said, dropping the scope into his EMT bag on the table. "Everything seems fine. Are you sure it's not the extra stress? I hate to say be that guy but look what happened to your house. And your car. You did have a fall, and raised pressure can do a lot of things to your brain."

Miles had not told Tommy everything. He had not said he had seen—had *thought* he'd seen—Diana do impossible things. He had said enough though, enough to make Tommy concerned about hallucinations. He'd said Abby had disappeared in a flash of light—an electric violet burst that no one else had seen. That he'd no idea where she'd gone—or why the light had seemed to touch only her. How its proximity had felt on his skin. Miles had nearly convinced himself it

149

was a head injury, that he had not truly seen those things at all. He hadn't been right since the night of the storm, when he'd woken on the floor of Bad Medicine Books & Herbs. He was certain there was an easy explanation for it all. But the dreams had begun before the rest.

He'd not expected his longtime friend to say nothing appeared wrong with him. He did not understand how something could be more wrong than ever, and yet not show a single sign. And he certainly did not expect to not be believed.

"Abby is missing, Tommy. I didn't imagine that."

Tommy crossed his arms. "I get what you're saying, I do, but maybe what you think you saw is not actually what happened." He shrugged and dropped his arms. "We see it all the time."

Dread settled in Miles's gut. If Abby wasn't found, and no one credited his story outside the fact that he was the last person to see her... Well, keeping his job would be the least of his problems. "Why was she even there?" he asked helplessly. "She said something about Chip asking her to look for me."

"No way," Tommy argued. "Chip didn't tell her anything. She overheard us talking is all." He shook his head. "I can't believe she showed up there. That's crossing some serious lines, even for her." Miles didn't comment on Abby's interference with his social life, but Tommy didn't need backup once he was on a roll. He flipped a toothpick out of his shirt pocket and rolled it between his fingers. "She needs to get over her beef with that Coulton girl. Since grade school, man. Can you imagine?"

Miles's gaze shot to his friend's. "Diana?"

Tommy shook his head. The overhead lights washed out

his features, making him appear thin and gaunt, not like himself at all. "Not Diana," Tommy said. "The younger one. Belle." He glanced out the door to be sure no one was coming, even though they'd done their makeshift medical exam in a disused office beside the storage rooms. "Man, that girl was somethin', even back then. She had those dark eyes and that black hair, but there was something about her that just said *fire*." Tommy smiled. "Not that you'd be into that."

Miles glared at him. "You forgetting you were in the middle of a story?"

Tommy laughed. "Right. So, anyway, Abby had a crush on this guy—man, I can't even remember who. I think the kid must have moved away that year or something. But he was nothin', really, just a random kid. And here was Abby, most popular girl in the school, always used to getting her way, and I mean, like the polar opposite of Belle in every single way."

"And Belle stole her boyfriend."

"That's the thing," Tommy said, spinning the toothpick between thumb and forefinger. "Abby hadn't even gone out with the guy. They were just kids." He held up a hand to indicate a height, then shook his head. "She'd just claimed him. Every boy was hers, you know?" Tommy's gaze took on a faraway look. "Then here came Belle, and all that was over."

"You're saying Abby drove all the way across town to find me because more than a decade ago, a little girl stole her grade-school crush?"

Tommy shrugged and leaned a shoulder against the metal racks that lined one wall. "I'm just saying. All guys are hers."

Miles frowned. "I was never Abby's."

Tommy gave him that patented smirk and tucked the toothpick into the corner of his mouth. "Doesn't mean she knows that."

Miles tried to recall a time when Abby had seemed interested in him, some indication that Tommy's assumptions were right. But it didn't fit. Abby had never so much as smiled playfully at him or leaned a little too close. She'd never crossed a single professional line.

Until she'd overheard he was staying with Diana.

His fingers curled into a fist. "It doesn't make sense. If there's nothing wrong with me, if my head is fine, then why do I know she's missing? She was definitely there. Now she's not and no one can reach her. And what about the rest?" He didn't have to say his obsession with Diana. The fact that he was less worried about Abby than a woman he'd just met was not lost on his friend. He might not have been able to speak his fears about the unnatural things he'd seen, but he'd tried to explain that his brain had been on a loop ever since that first day. "Why can't I stop thinking about her?"

Tommy chuckled. "Dude, that's easy. It's called *love.*" He leaned forward to give Miles a punch on the arm. "You're in deep."

Miles opened his mouth to argue. He had only just met Diana. Days, he supposed, if he counted the dreams. But raised voices echoed through the hall and Tommy's demeanor shifted instantly, the way it did when he responded to a call.

They strode down the corridor, then into the common area that separated the EMT and fire department garage from the county official offices.

Miles stared in shock. It was Abby, a bit windblown and

maybe rained on—though he'd thought the forecast had been clear—but apparently alive and well. She stood at the center of a half-dozen firemen, the only personnel on site since it was after hours, as she angrily protested their apparent lack of subordination.

"Right now," she demanded, pointing at anyone who made eye contact. "Get him on the phone *right now*. I want an entire fleet of officers at the Coulton house rounding up those horrid witches by dawn."

Miles went cold.

The word *witches* had shot ice through him. He wasn't even sure if she'd meant it as an alternative to a curse, but his feet were frozen to the ground, his body shivering. He could not seem to move from his spot.

Abby saw him anyway.

She called him out, that pointing finger leveling on him, and half the crowd's gaze followed along. "You," she said. "Miles saw them. He saw what those women did."

Beside him, Miles felt Tommy's presence, and he knew, despite every doubt he had voiced in private, Tommy would never tell the others what Miles had said. That he was so very concerned about the manner in which he believed he'd seen Abby disappear.

Or that he'd been unduly interested in one of the very Coulton women she'd accused.

"Tell them," Abby demanded.

Miles stared at her, expression blank.

He did not understand why he was not defending Abby, why he was not admitting that something was truly wrong. That something had indeed happened and he'd witnessed it with his own eyes. But he couldn't seem to act.

One of the guys lifted a wool throw to wrap Abby's shoulders, trying to soothe her the way they settled down patients. She screeched, the "*No*," echoing through the space as she tossed the throw to the ground.

The shop suddenly went dark.

Miles felt cool night air hit his skin as a half dozen flashlights flared to life around Abby. Her glare cut into his, and she made a declaration that she would *watch those women burn.*

Heat rose through Miles, melting away whatever had frozen him to the spot. He would stop her. If it was the last thing he did, Abigail Brown would never touch a—

"Dude, what is with these storms?"

Tommy's voice snapped the atmosphere between them and Miles startled back to himself. The crowd around Abby split. Half the fire crew moved away, muttering about backup generators and downed power lines, and the other half moved in, insisting she calm down.

Tommy took hold of Miles's arm, his gaze uncharacteristically wary. "Hey, man, let's get out of here."

TOMMY SHOVED Miles into his classic Camaro and backed out of the parking lot of the darkened city building complex. Miles leaned into the vinyl seat and pressed his head against the cool window. It vibrated against his skull as Tommy accelerated onto the main road, the black shadow of unlit security lamps striping the drive beneath the light of the moon.

The sky was clear. Not a night for power outages.

"Must be the wind," Tommy said over the sound of the engine.

Miles nodded absently, unable to take his eyes off the shape of the moon. He remembered staring up at it only nights before, full and bright. It had almost seemed to call out to him.

To whisper her name.

"Miles," Tommy called, evidently not for the first time given the annoyance in his tone. "Snap out of it, man."

"Yeah. It's fine. I'm good." Miles sat up as the neon of a retro drive-in diner lit the interior of the Camaro. The diner was Tommy's favorite spot for food, not because he was into corn dogs and milkshakes but because Tommy was into anything that gave him more time in his car.

Tommy glanced at Miles. "The usual?"

Miles nodded as Tommy coasted into a spot at the far end of the lot. He hit the headlight switch and shifted into park. Staticky doo-wop crackled through the car as Tommy cranked the window down by hand, and a brunette sauntered across the lot. Tommy drummed his thumb against the steering wheel while he waited. He wouldn't say anything while she was within earshot, but Miles wasn't sure his friend would have regardless. Tommy tended to allow Miles space until Miles gave him an opening.

Miles tried not to think about Diana. He tried not to remember how he'd seen her in dreams before he'd ever met her. How he'd woken and felt like she was there.

How he'd lain awake in her living room, unable to believe it was real.

How she'd come to him in the night, moonlight dancing over her bare skin. *Yes*, she'd told him. *Yes*. As if she'd been waiting to give him permission, to truly let him in.

The brunette stepped around a parking pole, then

leaned against the menu board, popping her chewing gum. "Hey, Tommy. What tonight?"

"Two number twos and one black coffee."

She nodded then tucked her pencil behind her ear as she spun to walk away. Tommy turned to Miles. "No coffee for you, man." He shook his head. "Not tonight."

Miles glanced down at his shaking hands. He curled them into fists. It was as if... as if he was having withdrawal. He pressed a fist to the center of his chest. He did not understand what was happening, but he knew its source.

"These burgers don't usually give you heartburn before you eat them." Tommy's remark was delivered offhand, but it was clear he was concerned.

Miles looked at his friend. "Something's wrong."

"No shit. It's about time you admitted it."

It was bigger than Tommy suspected. Far bigger than a bump on the head or some kind of infatuation with a woman, but Miles didn't explain. He only admitted, "I don't know what to do."

Tommy shrugged. "You'll figure it out. It's what you do." When Miles didn't respond, Tommy added, "I've never seen you like this, man. Maybe it's time you faced it head on."

Miles felt his heart race at the idea of going back. Terrifying things had happened. Unreasonable, illogical things. He maybe never wanted to set foot in that shop again. But, Diana. He could go back for her.

It was dangerous, in so many ways. But he knew he would. After the week he'd had, he wasn't certain *unsettling* or *unnatural* covered what he felt, but something had changed in him. He could not seem to *want* to stay away from her.

He could not seem to speak the words to tell his friend no.

Tommy took the silence as agreement. "Right, I'll drop you there." He smacked a palm to his stomach, evidently unaware of the cosmic shift in Miles. "After dinner though. This bad boy's gotta eat."

20

Diana stood in the back of the darkened shop, staring across the space. Moonlight through the stained-glass door dappled the floor with color. The sweet scent of bergamot lingered on the air. She wondered if this was the last night she would spend alone in Bad Medicine Books & Herbs.

Bernie had gone home to search the spell books for anything that could help their situation. Belle had gone to meet with a contact who had connections at the city, just to be sure they had warning should the fire-and-pitchfork mobs show up at their door. Diana should have been getting her affairs in order in the event their worst-case scenario proved true.

In case they were forced to run.

To leave everything behind.

She pressed a palm to her breastbone. Even the thought caused her physical pain. But there was more to it now. More that she did not want to leave behind.

There wasn't just the shop and their family home.

There was Miles.

Miles, who she'd only brought pain to. Who she'd only given trouble and distress. Miles, who would be better off had he never set foot into their lives.

Miles, who had traced a fingertip so lightly over the lines of her face. Who had stared at her in the moonlight and pressed his lips so gently to her skin.

Diana swallowed hard as she shuffled the papers on the countertop into a semblance of order. She snatched a pencil out of the cup, fresh and sharp, and began a new list: *Things to pack.*

The rumble of a loud motor echoed through the front windows, and Diana thought absently that it must be Belle. She did not give a second thought to what man might be dropping her sister off. Belle was right. It didn't matter.

Permanence was not for witches.

The bell above the door dinged, but Diana did not turn around. She didn't think she could look at either of her sisters and keep her emotions in check. Not tonight.

She scratched out the last item she'd noted then listed two more. It was hard to narrow down what was most important in life, what you'd take if you only had so much space and time. Prue glanced up from her spot on the floor. The tip of her tail flicked before she fell back asleep. Diana scribbled down *trunk beneath workroom counter, Aunt Cilla's worry stone.*

She felt Belle looking over her shoulder at the packing list.

"Going somewhere?"

Diana froze, her heart in her throat.

It had not been Belle's voice. It had not been Belle's presence she'd felt behind her. It was not, in fact, Belle, who was now leaning so perilously close to her she could feel his pulse thrumming with her own.

The lead of her pencil sheared against the paper beneath it.

Miles.

Diana turned, ever so slowly, into the electric atmosphere that surrounded Miles. That *was* Miles.

He watched her, expression unfathomable, but Diana's voice was lost, stolen away, dried up, and swallowed whole.

He kept watching her, not moving closer but not backing away. She had no idea what he was thinking, only that it did not appear to give him pleasure. His breathing seemed to steady, to fall into sync with hers. She felt it too, the way his presence seemed to calm her when she was anxious, even if her heart fluttered like the hexed moths every time she looked at him.

It was as if they needed to be near each other. Like they *belonged* together.

"No," Diana whispered. She shook her head, trying to move back, but the counter was behind her, trapping her. *This isn't right*, she wanted to say. *It's the hex. The spell is trying to shove us together, to tell us that we fit.*

She couldn't do that to Miles. She couldn't hurt him even more.

He reached for her, but she flinched away. He dropped his hand. "Are you leaving, Diana?"

The sound of her name on his lips was painful, but Diana could only shake her head. The situation was clearly not what he was expecting to find. "I have to. We—it doesn't —it's not okay anymore. We have to go."

"We?" Miles said.

"We have to leave. Move. It's the only thing that will fix it," she managed.

She tried to shift, to gather distance from him, but couldn't seem to get it done. Miles must have been having the same problem, because he seemed surprised to find his hand on her elbow. He stared at her, brows knit.

"I know," she told him. "I'm so sorry, Miles. I know you don't understand." She pressed her eyes closed. "If we just leave—that's all we can do. We can leave and maybe it will be okay." She was perilously close to tears.

Miles drew her to him, near enough she could feel the heat of his body. Too close, and yet she wanted nothing more than to be closer still.

"Tell me," he begged. "Tell me what this is."

Diana let out a long breath and opened her eyes. He was so near. It felt so *right*.

She was going to crush him and the thought of doing crushed her as well.

"What you saw, what you feel, Miles, all of that is because of me."

He didn't run from her like he'd done before, but she could see his concern. He knew what he'd seen—the lightning, the toads, all of it—was impossible, that something was terribly wrong. He just didn't know what.

She took a steadying breath then straightened to face him. "There's something very important I need to tell you. Something that could change everything." Her palms sweat at the idea that the words they'd been warned to never speak were about to come but she pushed on. Diana owed it to the man whose life would be destroyed by a curse. Neither of them would accept that what they were feeling was due to a spell without admitting this one truth. She didn't just owe it to him, she owed it to them both.

She wet her lips. "Miles," she whispered, "I'm a witch."

He leaned closer, as if maybe he hadn't heard, lips parted to speak.

Miles didn't speak. He only stared at her. She could feel him tremble, feel the emotion of a man who'd been nothing but steady since she'd first met him rattle through the room.

Witch, it seemed to echo.

Witch.

Diana had to show him. He needed to understand fully so he would see the other times had not been a trick of the light or a result of being knocked out. She would show him and would see. Then he would run.

This time, when he was sure of the truth, he wouldn't come back.

She took a steadying breath, lifted a hand between them, and twisted her fingers to trail a swirl of black smoke.

Miles jumped back, maybe not from Diana, but certainly from what was trailing her hand.

He stared at her, lips parted, still mute.

She frowned. "It's me," she insisted. "This is who I am." She rolled her palm open and let chamomile petals fall into it.

Miles gaped at the flower petals, then glanced up, above Diana's head all the way to the ceiling, leaning to one side as he searched for the source. Evidently, he would not be so easily convinced.

She made a fist then threw the petals, hissing the words that would turn them to ash.

Miles stumbled farther backward.

"A witch," she said again. "Don't you get it, Miles? None of this is real." She gestured between them helplessly to encompass the pain and yearning that felt as if it could tear her apart. "The curse did this. A stupid, drunken hex." She shook out her hands then brushed them over her jeans. "And now it's done and there's nothing I can do about it." She stared at him, willing him to understand, willing the sting of unshed tears away. "We have to leave. It's the only way to stop what's coming."

The blood had drained from Miles's face, but he'd still not managed a single word. She couldn't blame him, she guessed; it was a lot to process, but she found herself annoyed anyway. "Are you not getting it? The whole thing is a hex." She grabbed a pile of wilted rose petals that had gathered on the counter while she worked and shook them at him. They were nearly black, withering and dry. Time had run out. "A stupid, stinking love spell."

And that was it. That was the thing that finally broke his trance. He straightened, face flushed, and said, "You did this?"

She threw her hands up. "Yes. That's what I've been saying again and again."

He stepped forward. "No," he told her. "You did this? All of this?" She opened her mouth to agree, but he didn't let her. "*You* were the reason I hit my head? The storms?" He took another step toward her. "My house? This... this—" Miles's hand was pressed to his chest, and he looked as though he was in serious pain.

Diana felt sick. It was hurting him already. She knew it drew her expression into something horrid, because Miles's tone fell into a whisper.

"You took Abby?"

She stepped toward him. "No, I—" But she had, hadn't she? If not for her and her sisters, Abby would never have disappeared. She would never have come to the shop looking for Miles, never have tried to drag him away. "It was the spell," she told him. "It—it just got out of hand. We tried to stop it and—"

"What are you saying?" he snapped. "That you started this and now you can't control it?"

The guilt was on her face, even if it was not technically she who had done it. Bernie might have chanted the words, but Diana's heart had been the driving factor.

Diana had been the one to try to interfere with a spell already cast.

"I'm so sorry," she whispered.

Miles dropped his hands and stared up at the ceiling, but whatever he meant to say did not come. He stood frozen, some new emotion washing his features. He shifted slightly toward Diana, not taking his eyes from the ceiling, not moving anything aside from his feet.

Diana held her breath, following his gaze upward. She groaned and closed her eyes against the horror that was covering the stamped metal tiles.

Beside her, Miles whispered, "Tell me you're not doing that."

She sighed. "We should probably go outside until my sisters get back."

Miles was pressing his shoulder against hers. She didn't think he even realized; the hex was just drawing him in. She reached for her bag on the counter to call Belle. Her cell phone dropped to the floor when the door to the shop slammed open. Miles and Diana both jumped, the shifting mass of creatures on the ceiling suddenly the least of their concern.

Abigail Brown stood in the doorway of Bad Medicine Books & Herbs, moonlight casting her into horror-movie silhouette.

"You," she hissed, "are finally going to pay."

21

———

Diana stared at Abby, contemplating a few of the darker suggestions Belle had made to deal with the woman before they left town. Diana had argued then, but suddenly those plans gained a good deal of merit.

Behind the woman in question shifted two figures, hulking and uniformed. The type of men who could bring the downfall of women like Diana, Bernie, and Belle.

Miles stiffened beside Diana, and she managed a sharp, "The shop is closed."

Abby reached up and hit a switch that flooded the storefront with light. The cloud of bats that had been clinging to the ceiling swirled down and toward the door.

Diana could do no more than cringe as Abby shrieked and ducked, throwing up her arms to cover her head, her manicured fingernails noticeably dinged from the day's earlier events. The two men behind her leapt back, dodging the inky mass of wings. Abby howled her rage, throwing herself hands-first onto the floor in front of her to glare up at

Diana. She was practically on her knees, hair askew and makeup smeared when she howled, "What is *wrong* with you?"

Diana stared back, unable to form a response. She wished, more than anything, that her sisters were there. That she had the slightest idea what to do.

Abby crawled to her feet, shoving her pencil skirt back into place in a precise line just above her knees. The men behind her came forward again, eyes wary. One was wearing a white button-down shirt and tie with black uniform slacks, the other the dark blue of the local police.

This was it, Diana thought. Her sisters had been right. They should have already been gone.

She was going to destroy everything.

Just because she couldn't leave Miles.

She shook her head, frowning. Not Miles, the shop. Her family. Their home. Of course that was what she'd meant.

"You," Abby screeched, pointing a bony finger at Miles. "You're in on this, too. You saw what she did to me, and you'll admit it right here and now or suffer the consequences."

Diana swallowed hard, but Miles did not move.

He stood silently, staring on at what Diana was realizing with horror was probably the fire chief, his boss. Miles seemed to weigh his answer. As if he was deciding. As if he was considering whether to turn Diana and her sisters in.

She wanted to cry.

It was over. All of it. Everything.

"Tell them," Abby screamed.

"No." Miles's gaze distinctly did not flinch or stray toward Diana. "I was there, just like you said, but Diana Coulton was nowhere near at the time it happened."

He was protecting her. Yes, it was true that Diana wasn't on the street with them, but Miles knew it was her fault.

He was going to go down with their ship. He would lose everything that mattered to him when the truth came out.

When they were caught.

The men stared at Miles. They did not look at Diana. No one did.

It was as if she was invisible, had faded herself into nothing. She prayed she had not. She could not allow herself to slip and use magic again. Not with so many witnesses.

Abby's fists flung down tight against her sides, and she growled like an actual feral dog. "He's lying!" She stamped her foot. "Arrest that woman. *Now.*"

"Miss Brown," the officer beside her said calmly, "while I understand you've endured a harrowing experience, the fact is we do not have a single shred of evidence against Miss Coulton or a witness to the crime—including yourself." At Abby's glare, he added, "Per your signed statement earlier this evening, you cannot recall exactly how you left the scene."

"*She* did it. Everyone knows she's responsible," Abby whispered in a menacing tone.

"Nevertheless," the man said, "until we have a chance to further investigate the event—"

Abby threw up a hand to silence him, not bothering to rename it an actual *crime* despite her obvious annoyance at his merely calling it an event. "Fine," she spat. "Then how about you arrest her for those rabid bats? Does that work for you, Mister Proper Procedures Only?" She crossed her arms. "Since apparently kidnapping is not enough."

A "Ha!" came from the back of the room, and every head snapped in the direction of the darkened corridor. Out walked Belle, cold and sauntering, dark eyes cutting daggers through Abby from across the room. "Kidnapped," she scoffed. "You were gone for a few hours, and you can't even say where you went or how you got there. Seems convenient, don't you think?" Belle gave one of her best smiles to the police officer. Diana wanted to sink into the floor. "Did she tell you she came here afterward? Busted right in through the back door and tried to attack us on our own property."

Abby gasped, her outrage only serving as evidence against her—an admission of guilt.

Belle clicked her tongue. "I'm not sure what's been going on, boys, but it seems someone's been playing pranks on the women of Bad Medicine." Belle sidled up to Diana, gesturing a thumb toward Miles. "That's why we called Mr. Wieland, see. Abby's accusations first, and now this thing with the bats." She shook her head. "People have been trying to run us out for years with outlandish stories. Seems like grown adults would have something better to do with their time."

She let her gaze fall to Abby, then gave her a slow smile.

Abby screamed.

Everyone stared at her, awed at the way her composure had completely collapsed. Then Abigail Brown lost what was left of her control.

She rushed Belle in a rage, vile curses tearing from her as she leapt across the space.

Diana acted on instinct, moving in front of the enraged woman, though had she had a moment to think, she would have realized she'd been better off stepping back and letting her sister handle the fisticuffs. Because when she heard Belle's whispers behind her, Diana knew it had gone much too far.

You did not hex someone for spite.

You did not influence their actions.

You did not hex inside a hex, for fear of what might come back on you.

Belle was breaking all their rules.

Abby slammed into Diana's outstretched palms, clawing past her in an attempt to reach Belle. Miles stepped forward to grab the woman, but Abby's fury had pushed her over the edge. She jerked away from Miles, knocking Diana square in the jaw with an elbow. She swung a wild punch over Diana's back but wasn't near enough to strike Belle.

Belle smirked, egging her on for their audience, though Abby had already worked herself into a state. Diana was actually beginning to feel a bad sorry for her. The men at the doorway rushed forward, but Abby turned and, unable to get to Belle, grabbed Miles instead. She clawed into his shirt, yanking him toward her bared teeth.

"You," she seethed. "You will pay for this if it's the last thing I do." She jerked hard, snapping buttons loose. When Miles forcibly removed her hands, Abby's fingernails nicked the skin of his chest.

Time slowed, and Belle and Diana could only watch in horror as a drop of Miles's blood spilled onto the floor. It was the only rule worse than the others. The only thing that could cause the hex to turn again. *Blood.* Diana fell to her knees between Abby's heels and Miles's boots, her fingers pressing helplessly to the drop as it turned as black as a wilted rose, then soaked through the wood.

Belle was suddenly beside her, their fingers twined as they watched the spot on the plank fade from black to red to brown. Their eyes met.

Belle's held an apology that she had no time to voice.

Diana knew hers were only a reflection of her fear.

Darkness swept the showroom, sudden, heavy and choking. Abby, the fire chief, and the police officer froze where they stood, paralyzed by a foreboding they had no way to understand. Miles stared down at Diana and her sister, his white shirt stained with a thin line of blood.

Crisp, dried petals blew over the floor, settling between them in a pile of roses, the color of Bordeaux and ink. Their time was up. The curse had turned. Shelves lining the walls shook, bottles rattling and glass jars shattering on the floor. The air smelled of calendula and thyme. Of the end of things that were and the start of things to come.

Belle closed her eyes to focus her energy. Miles widened his stance, only bringing him closer to the women on the floor.

Belle began to sing, softly at first, a sweeping melody that prickled Diana's skin. It built, growing stronger, and Diana squeezed her sister's hand as she began to hum along. She needed to clear her mind, to focus on what mattered, what their intent truly was. But Diana could barely manage to breathe, let alone sort out her head. Miles, the shop, their safety, their freedom. There was too much wrong, too little time.

The candelabra display lit, flickering to life at the same time frankincense oil spilled over the floor. Abby and the fire chief watched in disbelief. The policeman put a hand first on his gun then his radio. He brought neither to bear.

Miles only had eyes for Diana. He bent lower, his knees touching the floor. "Diana," he whispered, understanding that she was afraid, that this magic was not hers.

Asking her what he should do.

He reached for her, took her free hand in his. The touch grounded her but not from the hex. It was Miles.

Only Miles.

Suddenly, her intent was clear.

Diana knew what she had to do.

Then a candelabrum toppled onto the frankincense oil, and the whole plan went up in flames.

22

D iana's muffled shout went no farther than Miles's shoulder as he slammed into her, to knock her away from the fire. The move jerked her hand free from her sister's, and Belle was thrown off balance, singing ceasing as she fell onto her bottom to stare at the flames eating up the oil on the shop floor.

"Fire extinguisher," Miles was saying, shaking Diana by the shoulders as she watched Belle dodging the flames. Acrid smoke spread through the room, searching for an outlet and only finding the open front door. Abby coughed, waving a hand in front of her face. It wouldn't be long before she realized the fire had them trapped. "Diana," Miles snapped.

She looked at him, his brown eyes serious and steady.

"Fire extinguisher," he said again.

She pointed toward the back of the shop, where a wall-mounted unit waited beside the corridor.

And he was gone, leaping through flames like a fire-fighter, which, she remembered, he actually was. The fire chief covered Abby's face with a strip of cloth, while the police officer radioed the station. Code eleven-seventy-one. Code eleven-forty-one.

Diana stared at Belle, her heart a wild animal in her chest. "I have to save him. It's too late for us, but I can't—I just can't do this to Miles."

"You can't save him," Belle answered. "He's already made up his mind. He chose you."

Belle got to her feet, pulling Diana up with her just as Miles cut loose on the fire extinguisher with a loud hiss—and the overhead alarms started to blare. White dust billowed up from the floor, surrounding them and dousing the fire as the screeching alarms warned of smoke. Thanks to Abby's aggressive fire code addendums, two of the exit alarms were equipped with strobes, the flashing lights turning the scene macabre.

Miles let off the extinguisher as the fire chief shut down the alarms. As soon as it was quiet, the chief shouted, "Is anyone else inside?" and Prue shot from behind him, through his legs, and out the open front door.

"That was it," Diana said lamely. Nothing there but everything precious she'd ever owned. She sighed, resigned for whatever disaster the hex would throw at them next, then wished she hadn't even thought it when a strange rumbling started beneath her feet. All eyes were on the door Prue had just shot out of as Bernie's bright-red hair streaked in front of the shop windows. She blew through the open door, out of the moonlight and into the once again darkened shop, only to trip over a candelabrum on the other side of the entrance rug.

"I've got it!" she yelled, whatever she *had* spilling from her arms to fly through the air.

The fire chief flipped on the back set of overhead lights just in time to reveal Bernie landing very near the police officer's feet, sprawled face down with her arms outstretched.

Around her was the white dust of the fire extinguisher, too bright in the now-illuminated shop. Spread among it, like blood on snow, were a hundred fresh red petals.

Roses.

Again.

"Magnificent timing," Belle said to her sister's prone form.

Bernie looked up at them, glasses askew at the top of her head.

The police officer glanced at Miles then leaned down to help what he hadn't been warned was a dangerous woman to her feet. She dusted her jeans off, looking guiltily between Diana and the police.

Diana tried to warn her with her eyes.

Bernie cleared her throat. "I, uh..." She gestured absently toward the door.

"Yes," Belle said. "You tripped. No surprise given the disaster this woman brought onto us." She narrowed her gaze on Abby, who was apparently too stunned to defend herself.

"What happened?" Bernie whispered, taking her sister's hint to play along. It fell short of awe, but her audience had been traumatized sufficiently to not catch on.

"Fire," Miles said from behind them.

Diana's head whipped toward him, but Miles was watching Bernie with a particularly accusatory glare.

"Oh," Bernie told him. "That's over now." She nodded, smiling as her gaze shifted toward Diana. "Feel better?"

Diana stared back, jaw slack. She realized Bernie was

right. She didn't sense the hex. Whatever she had felt rumbling beneath her feet was gone. The hex's next deed had disappeared the moment Bernie had burst into the room.

Miles just behind Diana, but she could no longer feel that electric draw, the push to go to him. She couldn't say she didn't feel tethered to him somehow, but it was not the insistent press it had been.

Bernie nodded enthusiastically. "So now, whatever you decide, you know, it's all you." Her smile was broad. "I fixed it."

Abby blinked, looking between the watching fire chief and police officer. "What the hell is wrong with you people?"

Diana glanced at Miles, but his eyes were on the storefront windows, where lights strobed red and bright through the shop. The women—civilians by the officer's estimation—were shortly escorted outside. Diana and Belle stepped gingerly over the rose petals, unsure exactly what Bernie had done. Blood had been spilled within a hex. Even if her sister had figured out how to end the original spell, it might have been twisted into something else. Something even less predictable. Diana hoped it was something less nefarious. Bernie took her hand, and the sisters left their battered shop to stand on the sidewalk beneath a pale moon and what seemed an endless array of flashing lights.

Diana's heart thumped an unsteady beat as men rushed past them, checking the shop as the fire chief and policeman who'd called it in tried to explain the source of the fire. *Earthquake*, one said. *Explosion*, said the other.

Emergency services seemed to have no idea what they meant. The night had been quiet. The storms ceased. Nothing outside the shop had gone amiss.

Diana searched the chaos and for Miles. He was speaking to another officer, probably giving his report. She started toward him, but Belle held her firm. "Let him be," Belle told her. "Whatever he says is up to him."

Bernie only sneezed.

Diana watched Miles. He glanced up from his paperwork, his gaze immediately finding hers, but she wasn't able to read his expression before someone cut off her line of sight. It was a tall blond EMT. The man's finger passed through the air toward the three of them. "Officer Charles said one of you might need to be checked out." His tone said that did not seem to be the case.

"Officer Charles?" Diana said.

The EMT nodded and gestured toward the policeman who'd helped her sister off the floor. The officer gave her a small, awkward wave, and Bernie beamed at him, wiggling her fingers back.

Diana ran a palm over her face.

The EMT pursed his lips at the exchange. "I see."

Belle leaned casually against the ambulance, boots crossed at the ankles, as she let her gaze run over the man. There was a spark of recognition in her eyes. She said, "So, what kind of motor do you have in this beast?"

The man smirked and looked her directly in the eye. "Is this a distraction or are you hitting on me right now, Arabelle Coulton?"

She let her head fall back in a laugh, straightening then strolling toward him as she said, "Hitting on you? Oh, Tommy boy, there'll be no question when I do." She flipped his collar with a long finger on her way past, not looking back for his response. He watched her go.

"That one's dangerous," Diana warned.

The EMT turned to her. "Oh, I'm aware." He smiled. "We went to school together. I was just telling Miles about that kid she got into it with Abby over..." He stopped, annoyed or confused, Diana couldn't be sure, then explained, "I can never remember his name. I think he moved away that summer."

Diana and Bernie exchanged a guilty glance.

He shook it off. "Anyway. I guess that was the year your mom started homeschooling you. We didn't see much of the Coulton girls after that." One of the officers near Abby called Tommy's name, and he tipped his finger toward his head in farewell as he turned to go. "Too bad you all didn't stick around. Seems like excitement sorta follows you."

Excitement, Diana thought. This guy had no idea.

23

Diana woke to the late-morning sun coming in through the row of windows in the living room of their family home, one thought on repeat: *Miles is gone*.

He had left. In the chaos of the night before, she'd not even seen where. She'd not even been able to tell him goodbye.

It was over just like that.

Because he couldn't trust her.

Because she was a witch.

Because everything that had happened had been based on a lie.

They'd been too tired to clean the shop, so once their statements were signed and the women released, they'd only locked the storefront door, climbed into the sedan with a disgruntled Prue, and driven the six miles to their family home in the rising sun.

Diana had collapsed onto the sofa, too spent for even a shower, and Belle had curled up beside her, wrapping an arm around her as she wept.

For her part, Bernie had attempted to explain in vague details how she'd remedied the spell, but Diana couldn't seem to find the energy to listen.

And now, with no more than a few fitful hours of sleep, they were quiet as they dressed and prepared for the day. Diana had lingered in the bath long after the water had gone cold. It was the first time the shop had been closed for business, and she'd not even posted an apology or note as to why on the door. It didn't matter, she guessed, because by now news of the previous evening and the fire had spread. It would be no more than gossip—business as usual for everyone else—while Diana's world felt like it had crumbled. Just another random Friday for everyone but the Coultons. Diana pulled the drain plug, wondering how her life had been so irrevocably changed by a single Sister Saturday and refusing to dwell on whether it would ever feel right again.

She dressed in an old pair of jeans and a faded sweatshirt. Her wardrobe in the apartment probably smelled of smoke and she dreaded having to face what damage had been done in the daylight. But it was time. Diana had decided to stay, to not leave it all behind, and she would do what she must to get things back into shape.

Even if both she and the shop would need time to heal.

When Diana came into the kitchen, Bernie was waiting with fresh-baked pastries. Diana wrapped one into a napkin to tuck into her bag as Belle passed over a cup of tea then ushered her toward the door.

Prue pounced through the corridor in front of them, determined not to be left behind with no one but an overly friendly Husky to keep her company. Belle scooped up Tilly off the counter, propping the crested gecko onto her shoulder, where it nested between her hair and a loose black scarf.

They let Bernie drive, though it usually terrified Diana to do so. She felt drained of everything, having come so close to her worst fears.

She wished she didn't feel the need to be responsible, that guilt wouldn't eat at her if she just crawled into bed and covered her head with a blanket for a month or so. She pressed her cheek against the cool glass of the side window, closing her eyes as they crossed in front of the shop.

She couldn't look. She didn't want to see.

Bernie drove around back, shifted the car into park, and turned the ignition off.

They were waiting for her to be ready to go in. Diana sighed and opened the car door. Her sisters followed her lead, grabbing the buckets and gloves and supplies from the trunk and backseat. The trunk reminded Diana of Miles, the same way the interior of the car had. The same way the shop and her apartment would. He'd taken up so much space in her life the last few days, and it seemed as if he was every-where, even while she felt the hole in her chest where he had been. It didn't seem possible. And yet, there it was.

She slammed the trunk shut. "Okay Let's do this."

They spent the first hour carefully scooping up white powder and gathering Bernie's scattered rose petals.

"How do we safely dispose of these?" Diana asked Bernie.

Bernie held out a hand for the basket of flower parts. "Probably best if you let me."

Belle slung the dust rag she'd been using to wipe off bottles over her shoulder to stare out the front window. She made a clipped *hm* sound.

Bernie and Diana turned to see what had caught her attention.

On the other side of the glass was Miles, gesturing awkwardly.

"He wants to come in," Bernie whispered, nudging her sister with an elbow.

Diana's feet seemed rooted to the floor.

Belle chuckled, walking toward the door. "I'll get it." She crossed the shop, unlocking the door as Diana hastily ran a hand over her hair.

Diana glanced at Bernie, panicked. Her sister smiled, brushing a smudge from Diana's cheek with her thumb.

"Breathe," Bernie told her.

Diana did, and as her eyes came back to the storefront, that breath felt as though it was stabbing through her chest. Miles was with two others—a tall blond wearing sunglasses she was pretty sure was the previous night's EMT—Tommy —and a stocky man whose eyes roamed the shelves with a hint of both caution and curiosity.

Miles crossed the room, and Belle took up conversation with the other men. Diana wet her lips, having no idea what to say.

Miles came to a stop about a foot from her, his gaze searching her face. They stood where they'd been only the night before, Bernie's spelled petals nowhere to be seen. The curse nowhere to be felt.

"Hi," he said.

She breathed out. "Hi."

He gestured over his shoulder. "I thought you could use some help today. Cleaning up."

Bernie backed slowly away from Diana, as if they wouldn't notice her leaving.

"Is that okay?" Miles asked.

"What—" Diana's brow drew down, her voice weak. "Is what okay?"

"That they're here."

She stared at him for a long moment before she realized what he meant. The magic. The witchcraft. The fact that they didn't know. She felt her eyes prick with tears and nodded. "Is it—it's all right with you?"

The magic, she meant.

The fact that she was a witch.

"I'm not sure it matters," he told her.

She leaned toward him, not entirely meaning to, voice low when she asked, "Why not?"

He tilted his head down, bringing them painfully near. "Because after everything I've seen, I still can't seem to want to stay away from you."

She hiccupped a laugh. "I'm not sure that's a compliment."

He smiled a little sheepishly. "I assure you it was." Then his smile fell, and he glanced over his shoulder to make certain their audience was busy amongst themselves. "I'm curious about something though." She waited patiently. His gaze traced her face, lingering briefly on the faint bruise at the edge of her jaw before coming to rest on her eyes once more. It was clear that he wanted to reach out, to brush his finger over her jaw, to be certain she was okay. It was also clear that he had something important to say. "Why did you pick me?"

Diana stared back at him, this man who'd become nothing like a stranger, who had felt like a perfect fit in every manner possible, who felt as if he'd been created just for her. She glanced down at her fidgeting fingers, forced them to still and straighten at her sides. She would be honest with him about everything, from that moment forward. Even if it hurt her. He deserved at least that much. And besides, he was *there.*

He'd come back.

"I didn't," she told him. "Bernie sent a wish out into the world, an intent to find someone honest and loyal and a match for me in every way. Someone I could love." She let him have her gaze. "It brought me you."

Miles drew in a breath, seemingly staggered. His hand came to his chest, palm sliding over the worn cotton T-shirt. "I didn't—" He shook his head, smiled. "I guess that sounds like a pretty good compliment."

She lifted a shoulder. "It's only the truth." She glanced down again before forcing herself to look at him. This would be the hard part, the part that might hurt. "It's your choice now, Miles. No matter what happens. No one will force you to be a part of this. To be with me."

He reached up to run a thumb over her cheek. Careful of the bruise, he let his hand slide against her neck. "I'm already a part of this, Diana. And if you're giving me the choice, I choose you."

Her heart pounded in her chest, her hands coming up to curl into the hem of his shirt.

His brow lowered. "What's wrong?"

"It's only—I'm only wishing we were alone right now."

He leaned his head nearer and slid his thumb over her cheek once more. As if he couldn't stop touching her. "Why?"

"So I could kiss you."

Miles's smile was slow, and unbearably sexy, as closed the distance between them. His kiss, though, it was soft and careful, as if he didn't want to break the tenuous agreement they'd made. Like he didn't want to lose her.

The hex was gone and it hadn't taken Miles with it. She let out a breath, part palpable relief, part dreamy sigh, and Miles kissed her again. This time, she was sure. He did not want her to leave. She drew back, looking up at him to promise, "I'm not going anywhere."

Beneath her palm on his chest, Diana felt the last bit of Miles's tension ease. "That's good," he said. "Because I'm afraid I would have to follow."

EPILOGUE

Hours after help had arrived, the smoke and debris inside the shop nearly eradicated, Tommy and Chip managed to drag themselves away for their night-shift duties —taking with them only promises of repayment in the form of pizza and a few hastily bargained herbal tonics.

Belle leaned against the shop counter beside Bernie, watching her eldest sister with Miles. It had worked out after all, evidently. Belle didn't suppose she should be surprised. If Bernie had anything, it was a good heart. She would have never purposefully brought Diana pain with her intentions, even if it had been a close call.

Tilly skittered across the counter over the top of one of the old spell books Bernie had stacked into piles. Belle noticed the edge of a slip of parchment where it had been tucked inside, scrawled with Bernie's loose, looping hand. She drew it out, reading *ginger root* and *spring roses* among other ingredients doodled beneath looping hearts.

"Bernie," she said after a moment, holding the paper up

to her sister. "This note full of scribbles looks like your spell parameters. The code to your hex."

Bernie sighed, fist under her chin, as she stared wistfully at Miles and Diana while they straightened the floral arrangements across the room. "Yeah, I know. I found it a few days after the spell was set."

Belle blinked.

Bernie glanced at her with a shrug. "They just seemed so right for each other. I didn't want to ruin it by letting her know." She shook her head. "Who knew they'd try to catch the shop on fire before accepting it. She's really stubborn, isn't she?"

Belle's mouth popped open, and Bernie straightened, immediately on the defensive. "It wasn't my fault. One of the letters found me." She glanced at Diana to be sure her sister hadn't heard. The faded notes had been arriving not entirely randomly in the years since their parents had been gone. They had never been signed, but the script had unquestionably been their mother's. They had offered love. Support. Thinly veiled advice. The sisters had learned long ago that if a letter suggested an action, it was best they took it. "Besides," Bernie said, "I didn't have the heart to tell her how to stop it." She frowned. "Look at them, Belle. They're just so perfect, you know?"

Belle did know. She'd never seen Diana so *right*. And, despite what she might tell Bernie, she was actually glad of it.

Belle knew her sister would need the strength that would come from a relationship with Miles. Because no matter how perfect the moment seemed, Belle understood what was to come for the Coultons.

She didn't need a faded letter to warn her. She'd seen it in the cards.

ALSO BY MELISSA WRIGHT

- STANDALONE FANTASY -

Seven Ways to Kill a King

RIVENWILDE STANDALONES

Beyond the Filigree Wall

Within the Hollow Heart

Upon the Riven Throne

- SERIES -

BETWEEN INK AND SHADOWS

Between Ink and Shadows

Before Crown and Kingdom

Beneath Stone and Sacrifice

THE FREY SAGA

Frey

Pieces of Eight

Molly (a short story)

Rise of the Seven

Venom and Steel

Shadow and Stone

Feather and Bone

DESCENDANTS SERIES

Bound by Prophecy

Shifting Fate

Reign of Shadows

SHATTERED REALMS

King of Ash and Bone

Queen of Iron and Blood

- WITCHY PNR -

HAVENWOOD FALLS

Toil and Trouble

BAD MEDICINE

Blood & Brute & Ginger Root

Visit the author on the web at

www.melissa-wright.com